HEY, IT'S RAFE AGAIN, BACK FOR MORE!

THIS TIME I'M GOING ON A WILD TREK INTO THE UNKNOWN.

• After all I've been through, been (mostly) **wrongfully accused** of, and been made to endure…

• I'm spending a week in the Colorado wilderness for a **lesson in survival**— if I can last that long.

• I have to deal with **screaming** Sergeants, raging rivers, and sagging shelters.

• Add in a snake girl, hard labor, and extreme hunger, and this is gonna be the **toughest week ever**.

• So what do I have to lose? Oh, nothing…except for my only chance of **ever** getting back into school!

You'd better buckle up, because starting now…

IT'S LIFE OR DEATH. GAME ON!

PRAISE FOR

"Wacky hijinks, a can't-miss setting and quirky characters keep this breezy story afloat. [It's] a **high-seas adventure** that will entice even the most confirmed of landlubbers."
—*Kirkus Reviews*

"A frenetic sense of excitement and adventure permeates this nautical escapade....There's little time to breathe as the Kidds pinball from one spot of trouble to the next, making for **a fun and fast-paced ride**."
—*Publishers Weekly*

"[The] illustrations are delightful—reminiscent of the elaborate doodles churned out in math class by **the most awesome artist** in seventh grade."
—*The New York Times*

PRAISE FOR
MIDDLE SCHOOL

★ "Patterson artfully weaves a... **thought-provoking tale** of childhood coping mechanisms and everyday school and family realities."
—*School Library Journal*, starred review

"Rafe is a bad boy with a **heart of gold**."
—*The New York Times*

"Will be enjoyed by middle-grade boys, **particularly reluctant readers**."
—*VOYA*

"A **perfectly pitched** novel."
—*Los Angeles Times*

PRAISE FOR
I FUNNY

A 2012 Dorothy Canfield Fisher Award Winner

"A brimming bucket of **bada-bing**!"
—*Booklist*

"Poignant...The affecting ending, which reveals a more vulnerable Jamie behind the guise of his humor, **celebrates Jamie's resilient spirit**."
—*Kirkus Reviews*

"Patterson [introduces] new jokes that **speak directly** to the middle school experience."
—*School Library Journal*

To Angela Galyean, Paul Lasher,
and the students of Hinesburg Community School
—C.T.

To Lilliana Rose Park and Baby Behan-Johnson.
I'm looking forward to knowing you both!
—L.P.

Copyright © 2014 by James Patterson
Illustrations by Laura Park
Middle School® is a trademark of JBP Business, LLC.
Excerpt from *Treasure Hunters* copyright © 2013 by James Patterson
Illustrations in excerpt from *Treasure Hunters* by Juliana Neufeld

Little, Brown and Company

Hachette Book Group
237 Park Avenue, New York, NY 10017
Visit our website at lb-kids.com

Little, Brown and Company is a division of Hachette Book Group, Inc.
The Little, Brown name and logo are trademarks of Hachette Book Group, Inc.

The publisher is not responsible for websites (or their content) that are not owned by the publisher.

First Edition: June 2014
First International Edition: June 2014

Library of Congress Cataloging-in-Publication Data

Patterson, James, 1947–
 Save Rafe! / James Patterson and Chris Tebbetts ; illustrated by Laura Park. — First paper over board edition.
  pages cm. — (Middle school)
 Summary: "Middle schooler Rafe Khatchadorian faces his greatest challenge yet as he struggles to complete a week-long wilderness survival course to prove to his school administrators that he can succeed" —Provided by publisher.
 ISBN 978-0-316-32212-6 (hardback) — ISBN 978-0-316-28629-9 (international) — ISBN 978-0-316-40599-7 (ebook) — ISBN 978-0-316-40598-0 (library edition ebook) [1. Wilderness survival—Fiction. 2. Self-reliance—Fiction. 3. Camping—Fiction. 4. Friendship—Fiction. 5. Humorous stories.] I. Tebbetts, Christopher. II. Park, Laura, 1980– illustrator. III. Title.
 PZ7.P27653Sav 2014
 [Fic]—dc23

2014002832

10 9 8 7 6 5 4 3 2 1
RRD-C
Printed in the United States of America

MIDDLE SCHOOL
SAVE RAFE!

JAMES PATTERSON
AND CHRIS TEBBETTS

ILLUSTRATED BY LAURA PARK

LITTLE, BROWN AND COMPANY
NEW YORK · BOSTON

CHAPTER 1

THE END IS NEAR!

Something tells me this story isn't going to have a happy ending.

I'm hanging on the side of a cliff by the jagged edges of my broken-off fingernails. The only thing between me and the ground is about half a mile of air, and I don't know how much longer I can hold on. Once I lose my grip—and I'm betting I *will*, any second now—it's going to be like taking the world's fastest elevator ride to the bottom. Without the elevator.

Good-bye, cruel world! Tell my mom that I love her. Also that there's a half-finished meatball sub under my bed. Knowing her, she's going to want to take care of that sooner rather than later.

This is it! The end of the line for me!

Except…wait a second. Here's the part where my whole life flashes in front of my eyes. And what do you know? Looking back, I guess I've been falling for a long time now.

Falling like Niagara.

Falling like my grades.

Falling like the leaves in…well, you get the idea. Just take a look. I don't have much time here.

It all started on the day I was born….

It didn't get any easier after that either. Mom said I had an "adventurous spirit" before I could even walk. Like for instance, the first time *this* happened.

And then there were the falls I never saw coming. Maybe I should have…but I usually didn't.

I mean, I know that everyone's life is supposed to have ups and downs. But for me, it's been more like ups and downs...and downs...and downs. I wouldn't have minded a few more *ups* once in a while. Sometimes I didn't have a whole lot of choice in the matter.

(probably the wrong way to put it. (You can guess what happened next, right?)

Miller the Killer
(Remember him?)

And just for the record, I want to say that not *all* of these disasters were my fault. Like for instance, this one was Jeanne Galletta's fault. (Technically.)

So I guess it makes sense that I'd wind up like this—dangling half a mile off the ground and waiting for gravity to turn me into sausage meat once and for all. I just wish I had a little more time. Then I might have a chance to prove I'm not a *total* loser.

But that's not going to happen. I'm down to my last fingernail, and there's no one around for a hundred miles to save me. I'm completely out here on my—

"HEY, RAFE!"

Wait a minute. That voice sounds familiar. Still, I can't believe it. I look up, and there she is—the last person in the world I expected to see.

"Georgia? Where'd you come from?" I scream. How did my little sister even get here that fast? It doesn't make any sense.

"Don't worry about that!" she says. "Just give me your hand!"

"I can't!" I yell. "If I let go of this branch, I'm going to fall!"

"Well, in that case," she says....

CHAPTER 2

JUST A DREAM

Hoo boy! That was a close one. Or at least, it sure felt that way.

I sit up in bed and look at Georgia standing there.

"I was having the craziest dream," I say. "There I was, hanging off the edge of a cliff, ready to drop. I even got to see my whole life flash before my eyes like they do in movies."

"Oh yeah?" Georgia says. "Did your recap include all of your colossal screw-ups? You got kicked out of Camp Wannamorra. You practically got kicked out of Cathedral School for the Arts. And don't even get me started about Hills Village."

"Yeah, yeah, thanks for the reminders," I say.

"You better hope Airbrook Arts School takes you back," Georgia says. "If not, then maybe you *should* start looking for a cliff, because Mom's going to kill you. You don't have too many chances left, Rafe."

My sister isn't just a world-class pain in the butt. She's also annoyingly smart. I never would have thought of it that way, but she's right. That nightmare of mine makes perfect sense.

"Oh, one other thing," Georgia says. Then she reaches under her chin, pulls back the loose flap of skin hanging there, and PEELS HER ENTIRE FACE RIGHT OFF HER SKULL!!!

CHAPTER 3

OKAY, *NOW* I'M AWAKE

Wow," Georgia said, standing next to my bed.
"Are you hard to wake up, or *what?*"

Or what. I still had a few more weeks of summer
vacation left, and I wanted to make them as good
as possible. And by "good," I mean as Georgia-
free as possible. She'd been home from Camp
Wannamorra for two whole days now, and that was
two too many, if you ask me.

Unfortunately, that morning, everything was
about to take a King Kong–sized turn for the worse.

"I have some bad news for you," Georgia said.
But I didn't give her the chance. I got out of bed
and shoved her right back into the hall where she
came from.

"Come back when I'm awake," I said.

"But you *are* awake," Georgia said as she started to push her way back into my room.

"Yeah, thanks to you," I grumbled. And then— *SLAM!* I shut the door in her face before she could get on even one more of my nerves.

Anyone want to bet whether or not that stopped her? (Spoiler Alert: It didn't.)

"Your school is closed!" she yelled from the hall. "Airbrook Arts is shutting down—permanently!"

See, this is what I mean about Georgia. Only *she* could think that was bad news. For me, it was more like the opposite—NO SCHOOL! And this was no dream either. This one was for real.

I turned right around and opened the door again.

"Seriously?" I said.

"Seriously," she said. "And Mom needs to talk to you about it, right now."

"Okay, but first—LOOK OVER THERE!"

"Where?" Georgia said, just before I whipped past her, ran across the hall and into the bathroom, and locked the door behind me.

"RAFE!"

Georgia absolutely hates it when I get to the bathroom first.

"Open up!" she said, pounding away. "I haven't even gotten to the real bad news yet. Are you listening?"

"NO!" I said.

"If you aren't listening, how could you answer me?" said my super-logical, super-brainy, super-loser sister.

"I'm busy! Just go away!" I said. It turned out that the bathroom wasn't such a great idea after all. Now I was trapped, and there isn't a door in the world that can block out my sister's voice once she gets going.

"Listen to me, Rafe!" she shouted. "Airbrook Arts is closed for good! Haven't you figured out what that means yet? There's nowhere left for you to go—except back to Hills Village."

That part hit me like a slow-motion hammer to the head.

"What?" I said. "Hang on...wait...what?"

I was pretty sure I'd heard Georgia right, but I

needed to be positive. If what she said was true, then I might have been better off falling from that cliff for real.

"You heard me!" she shouted on the other side of that door. "YOU'RE GOING BACK TO HILLS VILLAGE MIDDLE SCHOOL!!!"

CHAPTER 4

TOP TEN:
THE BEST OF THE WORST

Maybe you think I was overreacting. Or being crazy. Or both. But that just tells me you never read my first book. Because if you did, then you'd know that the worst years of my life all started right there at bad old Hills Village Middle School.

You might remember the crazy amount of rules that place had. You might also remember my plan to break all of them. After a bit of that, I sort of got kicked out.

I had a million reasons why I didn't want to go back to that place, but I won't bore you with all of them. Just the top ten. So here you go—

My Top Ten Reasons Why I Did Not (I Repeat, NOT) Want to Go Back to Hills Village Middle School!

NOTE: All-new pictures! Nothing borrowed or stolen from past books!

(Stolen? Me? Never...)

#10: NOT ALL MIDDLE SCHOOLS ARE CREATED EQUAL. If I *had* to be in middle school, at least Airbrook was going to help turn me into a real artist. The last time I was at HVMS, it helped turn me into a real criminal (and a big-time disappointment to my mom).

#9: VICE PRINCIPAL IDA P. STRICKER. Mrs. Stricker is in charge of discipline, misery, and suffering at Hills Village Middle School. And let's just say that she's *very* good at her job.

#8: JEANNE GALLETTA. Okay, don't get me wrong. At this point I was pretty much in love with Jeanne. But if you've ever been in love and happen to be as completely lame as me, then you know that the only thing worse than *never* seeing that person is seeing them *all the time*, when you have all kinds of chances to make yourself look about as smooth as a bowl of gravel.

#7: MATH…SCIENCE…ENGLISH…SOCIAL STUDIES. Do I even need to explain this one? Classes haven't exactly been my strong suit.

#6: RULES, RULES, RULES, RULES! Hills Village Middle School has more rules than anywhere I've been. (I think Mrs. Stricker has something to do with that.) When I was at HVMS before, I broke a couple (like maybe eighty-six of them...) and ended up getting expelled.

#5, 4, 3, 2, and **1:** MILLER THE KILLER. Let's just put it this way: The last time I came face-to-face with Miller, there was blood involved. If you're following the story so far, you can probably guess it wasn't his.

CHAPTER 5

BEWARE OF THE BACON!

Here's the deal in my house: When there's pancakes for breakfast, it means Mom doesn't have to work that morning and she has more time for cooking.

When there's bacon, it means Mom made some extra-good tips at the diner that week, because we can't afford stuff like that all the time.

But when there's pancakes *with* blueberries *and* bacon? That's when you have to watch out. Usually, it means there's some bad news coming for dessert.

Mom was flipping pancakes when I came into the kitchen. Grandma Dotty and Georgia were already there, sitting at the table and demolishing a couple of short stacks.

"Good morning, Rafe!" Grandma said. "Ready for an absolutely terrible day?"

Dotty's an awesome grandma, but you kind of have to get used to her. Like, just because she *shouldn't* say something doesn't mean she *won't* say it.

"Here you go, sweetie," Mom said, sliding a plate in front of me. "Fresh off the griddle."

"Thanks, Mom," I said. "Georgia already gave me the bad news about Airbrook. And about me going back to Hills Village too."

"Yes, well, that's what the pancakes are for," Mom said. "Kind of a consolation. I'm sorry, Rafe, I know how much you wanted to go to Airbrook instead."

Georgia piped up then, while passing Grandma Dotty some more bacon. "So then, what're the blueberries for?" she said. "What else is wrong?"

So I guess she'd figured it out too.

"Well..." Mom said. "I was going to wait until

after breakfast, but Rafe and I have a meeting at the middle school this morning."

"We do?" I said.

"I got an e-mail from the principal's office saying we need to come in and discuss a few things," Mom told me.

You might think that part would make me lose my appetite, but it didn't. I mean, come on! It was blueberry pancakes. I figured I might as well have an awesome breakfast first, and *then* go back to my absolutely terrible day. Because whenever some adult says they want to "discuss" something with a kid, you can bet your last piece of bacon it's not going to turn out great for the kid.

In the meantime, I didn't complain or give Mom a hard time. Why would I? She was barely done being mad at me about getting kicked out of Camp Wannamorra. When she and Grandma came to pick me up that day, I think she was about ready to drop me off at the trade-in center for a new son.

Instead, Mom gave me the silent treatment for a while, and then yelled some, and then worst of all, cried some too. If you know me, then you know there's nothing I hate more than seeing my mom cry.

The point is, even if I didn't like how things were going now, it was my own fault. I even felt sorry for Mom, having to deal with me all the time. I mean, if I had a kid just like me…

Well, actually, that might be kind of awesome. But still, I felt bad for Mom. She deserved way better. So I decided right then that I was going to do whatever I could to make this next part go right.

Hills Village Middle School, here I come. Like it or NOT.

CHAPTER 6

LOOK WHO'S HERE

Walking into a school in August is like walking onto a ghost ship. You feel like you shouldn't be there, and you're never sure who—or what—you might run into.

It was especially weird coming into HVMS. Nobody had to remind me where the principal's office was either. I could practically see my old footprints, wearing a path to Principal Dwight's door.

When Mom and I got to the admin center, the front part was empty but the principal's door was open. I figured Mr. Dwight was back there, sitting at his desk and waiting to yell at me about... whatever I was there to get yelled at about.

Except, it turned out I was wrong. Mr. Dwight *wasn't* at his desk.

Ida P. Stricker was.

"Hello...Rafe," she said.

"Did you and Mr. Dwight switch offices?" I asked, hoping like crazy for a *yes*.

"No," she said. "Mr. Dwight is no longer with us."

"He died?" Mom said. "That's awful."

"Actually, he won the jackpot on a Bucks for Life scratch-off ticket," Stricker said. "I think he's in the Bahamas right now."

"Oh," Mom said. "How nice for him."

"I suppose," said Mrs. Stricker, like she'd just bit down on the sourest puppy in the whole patch.

I never thought I'd be jealous of Mr. Dwight in a million years. But I sure was now.

"And how are you, Mrs. Stricker?" Mom asked.

"It's Principal Stricker now," she said. "And I'd like to get right to business."

She picked up her phone and pressed a button. "Charlotte? Would you come in here, please? And bring Rafe Khatchadorian's old file."

I could tell that even Mom was getting a little ticked off by now. "What is this about, exactly?" she asked.

"I'm going to let our new vice principal explain the details," Stricker said. "But to be clear, we're not here to discuss *when* Rafe will be returning. We're here to discuss *whether or not* he'll be returning at all."

"EXCUSE ME?" Mom said.

I felt like someone had just popped open my skull and thrown a firecracker in there.

Wha' jus' happen?

Stricker sat back in her chair. She might even have smiled, but with her, it's hard to tell. Let's just say that old Ida liked me about as much as I liked her.

"But you're required to enroll Rafe," Mom said. "This is a public school."

"Yes," Stricker said. "A public school from which Rafe was expelled not too long ago. That expulsion still stands, unless Rafe proves that he can abide by the rules."

"I can't believe this," Mom said. "There's nowhere else for him to go! There must be something we can do."

"There is," Stricker said.

Just then, a lady I'd never seen before walked into the office. She had a smile that was about as big and friendly as Mrs. Stricker's. It looked like this:

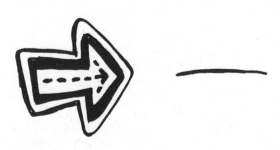

"You must be Rafe and Mrs. Khatchadorian," she said.

"Yes," Mom said, sounding more annoyed by the second. "And you are?"

When the lady reached over and shook Mom's hand, I'm pretty sure I heard some knuckles crunching.

"Vice Principal Charlotte P. Stonecase," she said.

CHAPTER 7

GET WITH THE PROGRAM

When I heard that name—Stonecase—I knew right away who she was. This lady was a legend.

"You teach at Airbrook, don't you?" I said.

"*Wrong*," she said. "I *used* to teach at Airbrook."

"Oh, right," I said. Airbrook Arts Community School was gone, gone, gone. *Duh.* That was what I was doing there.

I'd never met Mrs. Stonecase before, but at Airbrook, they called her the Terror from Room 666. She had a killer reputation and kept a real human skull in a jar on her desk. Supposedly.

"Mrs. Stricker says you have some idea about how Rafe can be re-enrolled?" Mom asked Mrs. Stonecase.

"What I have is an *opportunity* for Rafe," she said. "The rest will be up to him."

She handed Mom some kind of brochure.

"'The Program'?" Mom said, looking at the cover. "What is this?"

"A highly effective one-week intensive program for behaviorally challenged students." Mrs. Stonecase looked at me like I needed to be scraped off the bottom of her shoe.

In other words, this was something for screw-ups like me. I could only see a little of that brochure, but on the cover it looked like people were doing outdoor stuff, like hiking and rafting.

"Is it a camp?" I asked.

Mrs. Stricker and Mrs. Stonecase laughed. That didn't seem like a good sign.

"So you're saying that if Rafe participates in The Program, he'll be readmitted at the beginning of the school year?" Mom said, using her trying-to-be-patient voice.

"*Wrong*," Mrs. Stonecase told her. "We're saying that *if* Rafe participates—"

"—and *if* he completes The Program—" Stricker said.

"—*then* we'll consider re-enrolling him," said Stonecase.

Seriously, these two were starting to creep me out.

But that didn't even matter. I already knew I had to do this thing, no matter what. Not for my own sake. *For Mom's*. She deserved the best. And since I couldn't give her that, I'd have to give her *my* best.

Whatever it took.

"I'll do it," I said. "And I won't mess it up. That's a promise."

"All right, Rafe," Mom said, looking at me like she was mad, sad, and proud, all at the same time. "I have to talk with Mrs. Stonecase and Mrs. Stricker a little more about this. Why don't you wait outside?" She handed me the brochure.

And *that's* when I got my first real look at what I had signed up for.

The kids in the pamphlet weren't hiking. They were marching through the mud. And they weren't exactly rafting either. It looked to me like they were just trying not to drown. There was also some writing at the very bottom that I hadn't seen before. It said in boldfaced letters, "The hardest week of your life is about to begin."

As far as I could tell, that pretty much said it all.

I couldn't imagine what could be in store for me at The Program. I was kind of used to being a loser, sure, but I might need a miracle or two to make it through this one.

It was time for a little art therapy.

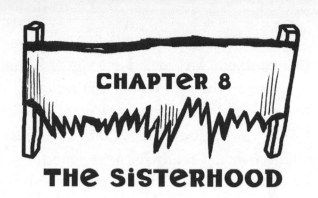

CHAPTER 8

THE SISTERHOOD

What are you working on there?" someone
said.

I slammed my sketch pad closed and looked up.
"Ms. D!" I said. I *thought* I was alone. While I was
waiting out in the hall for Mom to finish up with
Stricker and Stonecase, I'd been drawing to take
my mind off the nightmare I was about to face at
The Program.

Ms. Donatello was my favorite teacher when I
was at HVMS before. Not that there was a lot of
competition for that spot.

Now she was standing there in the hall with a
big armful of books and posters. "I just came in to
work on my classroom," she said. "And, Rafe, I'm so

sorry to hear about Airbrook. I see you're keeping up with your art, though. That's wonderful."

"Thanks," I said. I could tell she wanted to see what I was drawing, but I kept that sketch pad closed tight. I wasn't ready for anyone to see my Loozer comics yet, especially the parts about Leo the Silent.

Leo was my brother who died a long time ago, when we were practically babies. So in that way, he's a real person to me. Nobody can see him or hear him, but we still talk things through sometimes.

If you know my story, then you might have started wondering where Leo's been. I still talk to him, but mostly these days, I do it in my art. That seems like a pretty good place for Leo to hang out, right?

One of these days, maybe I'll start putting those comics online. Then Leo won't be a secret at all. In fact, maybe he'll even be famous.

But in the meantime, I was keeping that stuff to myself.

"So does this mean you'll be joining us back here at HVMS?" Ms. Donatello asked me.

"Uh...maybe," I said. "Mom's in the office, talking to Mrs. Stricker and Mrs. Stonecase about it right now."

"Ah, the Sisterhood," Donatello said, and winked at me.

"Huh?" I said.

"Ida and Charlotte are sisters," Donatello said.

"No way!" I said.

"Way," she said. "Did you notice they both have an initial *P* in their names? It stands for *Petaluma*."

And almost right away, it all started making sense.

The Sisterhood didn't think I could make it through this crazy *Program* thing, did they? They couldn't just keep me out of school for good, but they could make it really hard for me to get back in.

I mean, unless I was being totally paranoid and living in my own fantasy world on Planet Rafe.

I kept thinking about what it said on that brochure. "The hardest week of your life is about to begin."

But now I was also thinking, *Okay, bring it.* Game on, sisters!

"Hello?" Ms. D said, and waved her hand in front of my eyes. "Earth to Rafe, are you there?" When I looked up at her, she was staring back at me kind of funny.

"You know what?" I told Ms. Donatello. "Forget what I said before. I'll *definitely* be back here at HVMS this fall."

Because now I had *two* good reasons for doing this.

First, more than anything, I needed to make Mom happy.

But also now, if I *had* to go back to HVMS (and I

did), then I was going to make sure the Petaluma Sisters were just as sorry about it as I was.

So how weird was this? All of a sudden, I was fighting to GET BACK IN to Hills Village Middle School. Life is crazy sometimes, isn't it?

Maybe this game wasn't going to have a whole lot of winners, but if I played it right, then at least I wouldn't be the only loser.

LET'S GO TO THE MOVIES!

When we got home, Mom surprised me and gave me and Georgia twenty dollars to go to the movies. That was enough for food too. The only catch—obviously—was that I had to bring Georgia. I guess Mom needed some Mom Time.

"Hey, it's my twenty dollars too!" Georgia said when I wouldn't let her pick the movie (like I was going to sit through two hours of whatever lame movie she'd want to see) or the snacks (Twizzlers and popcorn, extra butter).

Then, when we walked into the theater, I noticed the last person I wanted to see when I was at the movies with my sister: *Jeanne Galletta*. I recognized the back of her head. And her laugh too, which sounds kind of like sunshine, I guess. I mean, if sunshine had a sound.

But then I figured out why she was laughing. She was sitting next to some guy, and they were sharing an extra-large popcorn and soda between them.

"Hey, it's Jeanne!" Georgia said, but I pulled her right into the back row before she could yell out and embarrass me.

"Shhh! She'll hear you. Who's that kid with her?" I said, trying to hide behind my Twizzlers.

"You know him," Georgia said. "That's Jared McCall."

"*That's* Jared McCall?"

The last time I'd seen Jared, he was shorter than *me*. Now he was someone you wouldn't even want to sit behind at the movies.

"Jeanne's so lucky," Georgia sighed. "He's supercute. And he plays lacrosse. *And* sings with a boy band at school—Jared and the Jaguars."

"Is that all?" I muttered. "He's not that great."

"Yeah, and you're not that jealous."

"Whatever," I said. "Have some more popcorn."

"You know, if you want Jeanne to like you, you're going to have to talk to her sometime. You get that, right?" Georgia said.

"Are you serious?"

"Of course I'm serious," she said. "You should just—"

"No, I mean, do you seriously think I'd take any advice from *you* about girls?" Then I gave her the whole thing of popcorn to hold, so she wouldn't talk anymore. But even that backfired. In about a minute, Georgia got up and handed it back to me.

"Take this," she said.

"Where are you going?" I asked.

"I'm going to ask Jeanne for a sip of her soda."

"No!" I said.

"I have to. That popcorn's making me super-thirsty," she said. "And besides, you're funny when you're worried about girls."

Before I could grab her and pull her back, Georgia was walking down the aisle. And then she was talking to Jeanne. And to stupid, perfect Whatshisname. And then—even worse—all three of them turned around and looked right at me.

"Hi, Rafe!" Jeanne said.

"Hey," I said, feeling totally stupid. Not because I'd done anything dumb, but because I probably would, any second now.

"Do you want to come down here and sit with us?" Jeanne offered.

No, that's not really what I said.

"I'm good," I said. "I think I, uh…need glasses or something. I can see better from back here."

And there it was—*dumb-dah-dumb-dumb-dummmmmb!*

Now even Georgia was looking at me like I was insane. "Suit yourself," she said, and plopped down next to Jeanne.

And that's when I realized that maybe Georgia wasn't *just* torturing me. Maybe she was also trying to help at the same time. But I'd just blown *that* opportunity, hadn't I? Way to go, Khatchadorian!

And I was starting to think maybe surviving out there in the wild was going to be the easy part. At least if I drowned I wouldn't have to watch *The Jeanne and Jared Show.*

CHAPTER 10

BRAVE...iSH

So, the movies were a disaster.

It turns out, once you decide you basically love someone, it gets a lot harder to act like a normal human being and make words come out of your mouth when they're around. It doesn't seem fair, but I guess a lot of stuff in my life hasn't exactly seemed *fair*.

And besides, Georgia wasn't totally wrong. If I wanted to impress Jeanne at all, I needed to get over myself and actually *talk* to her once in a while.

So on the night before I left, I picked up the phone and called Jeanne to say good-bye. Hey, if I could face a week in the wilderness with a bunch of strangers, I could make it through one stupid phone call, right?

(Yeah…I thought so too.)

It started out okay enough. At least I didn't hang up when I heard Jeanne's voice at the other end of the line.

"Hello?" she said. "Galletta residence, Jeanne speaking."

"Hi, it's Rafe," I said.

So far, so good.

"Hi, Rafe, what's up?"

"Well," I said, "I just…um…I didn't get a chance to tell you at the movies the other day, but I'm coming back to HVMS this fall."

"Yeah, I know," she said.

"You do?"

"Yeah, Georgia told me."

"She did?" I said. And then I was wondering what *else* Georgia had said.

Meanwhile, my brain was racing about a thousand miles a minute, while my mouth was stalled out at the side of the road. I couldn't figure out *what* to say next—until I remembered (DUH!!)

why I'd called Jeanne in the first place.

"So anyway," I said, "I'm going on this trip before school starts. No big deal, just a week in the Rocky Mountains. A little hiking, a little rock climbing, some highly dangerous white-water rafting—that kind of thing."

"Oh, really?"

"Yeah," I said.

And then there was this...big...long...silence. I kind of thought she'd have more to say about it than just *Oh, really?* But she didn't seem too impressed. With my luck, Jared McJockstrap had just gotten back from a thousand-mile swim up the Amazon River to deliver fresh food to hungry animals and give a live concert to the people of South America.

I probably should have waited until I got back and worried about impressing Jeanne later. But noooo, I just *had* to pick up the stupid phone and—

"Hello?" Jeanne said. "Rafe? Are you still there?"

"So...uh...yeah...okay...anyway," I mumbled.

Now what was I supposed to do? I'd run out of material. I didn't think I could wing something

without looking like even more of a doofus. I didn't know if I should keep going, or if we were done, or what.

So of course, I did the stupidest thing possible. I didn't say anything at all. I hung up.

That's right. I just...hung up. On the girl I was in love with.

Seriously, when it comes to being *bad* at this stuff, I am the absolute best there is. No contest.

If I ever figure any of it out, I'll let you know. In fact, I'll have a party and invite you. In the meantime, you're probably getting a good idea about why I call my comic *Loozer Loses Again*. Because I always do.

I mean—*he* always does. Again, and again, and again.

And again.

CHAPTER 11

HiTTiNG THE ROAD
(AND HOPiNG iT
DOESN'T HiT BACK)

At four o'clock the next morning (which is way too early for normal people), it was time to get on the road. Mom loaded up the car with me, my stuff, Georgia, and Grandma, and we took off for the Rocky Mountains, Colorado, USA.

The whole family was coming along because Grandma's brother Paulie lived outside Denver, so Mom, Georgia, and Dotty were all going to spend the week at his place. Georgia wasn't too excited about it, but she was getting a luxury vacation compared to me. I told her I didn't want to hear any complaining in the car. And believe it or not, I never did.

She'll be comin' round the mountain
when she comes. She'll be comin' round
the mountain when she comes. She'll
be comin' round the mountain, she'll be
comin' round the mountain, she'll be
comin' round the mountain when she
comes! She'll be riding six white horses
when she comes. She'll be riding six white horses
when she comes. She'll be riding six white horses,
she'll be riding six white horses, she'll be riding
six white
Just kill me now.
Adventure (and certain death) AHEAD

63

In fact, it was impossible to hear anything besides all the singing. It turns out Grandma Dotty just *loves* to sing in the car. She's like a human jukebox that only plays the world's oldest, corniest songs. You probably know some of them, like "On Top of Old Smoky" and "Camptown Races" and "Oh! Susanna."

While everyone else was singing their heads off, I spent my time drawing in my notebook, staring out the window, and rereading that Program brochure. I wanted to know *exactly* what kind of torture I was getting into here.

The brochure said it was going to be a seven-day, six-night "ADVENTURE" in the mountains.

By the time we finally crossed the Colorado state line, I must have read that thing a hundred and sixty times, and I was getting crazy-nervous.

I also had "She'll Be Comin' Round the Mountain" stuck in my head like a tattoo on my brain. I even made up my own version. It's called "Welcome to The Program," and you can sing along if you want. (Don't worry, your singing voice can't be any worse than mine.)

I was supposedly going to "CHALLENGE" myself and "DISCOVER" what it meant to be "ACCOUNTABLE" for my actions, through a "VIGOROUS" program of "PHYSICAL AND MENTAL OBSTACLES."

The brochure also made a big deal about leaving behind the "EVERYDAY COMFORTS OF HOME." I was pretty sure that meant pooping in the woods without toilet paper. And it definitely meant no computers, no phones, no video games—nothing. It literally said "NO ELECTRONICS" nine different times, in nine different ways.

The whole thing made me want to "TOSS MY COOKIES" every time I thought about it.

CHAPTER 12

NO WAY OUT

After thirty-one hours, twelve hundred miles, one night in a seriously creepy motel, eight rest stops, two coolers full of sandwiches, and one whole apple pie from Swifty's Diner...we finally got to the "rendezvous point" for The Program.

And no, it wasn't as cool as it sounds. It was just a dirt parking lot in the middle of the biggest nowhere you've ever seen. There was one Porta Potti, one yellow school bus with some people on it, and a guy in a cowboy hat and army fatigues standing outside.

Mom pulled in and rolled down her window.

"Are we in the right place for The Program with Rocky Mountain High?"

"Yes, ma'am," the guy said. "I'm Sergeant Fish. And this must be Rafe in your backseat."

"How did you know?" Mom said.

"'Cause you're the last ones here. And you're late. We're getting ready to head out."

Mom looked at her watch. "But you aren't supposed to leave until—"

"Eleven hundred hours, ma'am, yes, ma'am. It's now ten fifty-eight."

"But—"

"First lesson of The Program—be early to be on time," Sergeant Fish said.

"Ah," Mom said. "I see." Then she winked at me in the rearview mirror. She'd been reading about The Program too, and knew what to expect.

"Rafe, I'll throw your gear on the bus while you say your good-byes," Sergeant Fish told me. "But you need to make it snappy. Got it?"

"I guess so," I said.

I was getting it, all right. Anywhere they use words like *gear* and *eleven hundred hours*, you can be pretty sure you're not there for surfing lessons and make-your-own-sundae bars. I had plenty of time to figure out just how serious of a mess I was in.

What I *didn't* have was enough time to figure out HOW TO GET MYSELF OUT OF IT!!!

As usual, I had plenty of ideas, but not a single one that was going to do me any good. Everyone was staring at me and waiting for me to get a move on. All I could do now was step out of the car, hand over my stuff, and start figuring out how to survive the next seven days and six nights.

It was time to say good-bye.

CHAPTER 13

WHAT'S SO GOOD ABOUT GOOD-BYE?

This is it, kiddo," Grandma said, and gave me one of her famous bone-crushing hugs. "We'll see you in a week. Unless you don't make it that far, which you might not. I've seen that brochure too. But anyway, good luck!"

"Um...thanks?" I said.

"Yeah, good luck," Georgia said. "I think you're going to need it. That Sergeant guy looks like he could eat you for breakfast—"

"Come here, you," Mom said. She put an arm around my shoulder and walked with me away from everyone else, across the parking lot.

"YOU HAVE ONE MINUTE!" Sergeant Fish yelled after us.

"Yes, sir, Sergeant Fish, sir," Mom said, just loud enough for me to hear. "I guess we better make this good and 'snappy,' huh?" I think she was making jokes to try and calm me down, but she would have had better luck giving a back rub to a brick wall.

"Mom?" I said. "I don't know if I can do this."

Mom stopped walking then and looked me right in the eye. "Listen to me, sweetie," she said. "All I can ask is that you do your very best. And I'll tell you something else. I don't think either of us has seen that yet. You have so much more inside you, Rafe. You just need to see that for yourself."

Mom's pep talk wasn't making me feel very peppy, to be honest. Mostly, I felt confused.

"So...what does all that have to do with hiking and rafting and getting yelled at in the woods?" I said.

Mom smiled and reached over to give me a big long hug. Then she whispered in my ear, "That's what you're here to find out."

I guess that was the end of one minute, because Sergeant Fish started screaming across the parking lot again.

"TIME TO ROLL, KHATCHADORIAN! LET'S GO! MOVE LIKE YOU'VE GOT A PURPOSE!"

"That's your cue," Mom said. Then she started walking me toward the bus. "I love you, Rafe. No matter what," she said.

"Love you too," I said. I wanted to say more, but my throat was closed up tighter than Santa's workshop on December 26. And I definitely didn't want to start crying.

Mom didn't cry either, even though I thought she might. I think she was trying to show me she could be strong if I could. It was one more reason why she's basically the most awesome mom in the world.

Also—one more reason why I had to just shut up, buckle down, and get on that bus. After her speech, I wasn't going to let her down ever again, if I could help it.

CHAPTER 14

SARGE IN CHARGE

When I got on the bus, there was a lady sitting in the driver's seat. She had the same fatigues on as Sergeant Fish.

"Welcome aboard, Rafe. I'm Sergeant Pittman," she said, and then pointed at all the kids in the back. "That's Carmen, Arnie, Burp, Thea, Diego, D.J., and Veronica. Got it?"

I didn't really catch any of the names. I just noticed how everyone looked like they'd rather be taming rattlesnakes blindfolded while on fire than sitting on that bus.

Also, I couldn't help noticing that some of the guys in this program…were girls. I don't know why, but I wasn't expecting that.

"No talking until we reach base camp," Sergeant Pittman said. "Take a seat, Rafe. Sixth row on the left."

"Am I allowed to—" I said, but Fish was right there to shut me down.

"WHAT DID SERGEANT PITTMAN JUST SAY ABOUT NOT TALKING?" he asked me.

It seemed like a trick question. So I kept my mouth shut and just went to find my seat instead.

"ALL RIGHT, COCKROACHES, LISTEN UP!" he said. "We'll be at base camp in two hours. Settle in, keep your eyes front and your lips closed tight. Any questions?"

A couple of hands went up.

"Too bad! No talking until we get there!" he said.

In that Program brochure, they talked a lot about how much I was going to learn out here. And even though nobody's ever called *me* a fast learner, I'd already figured out that I hated Sergeant Fish more than asparagus, paper cuts, and pre-algebra combined.

And this whole thing was just getting started.

Ten minutes down. Seven days to go.

CHAPTER 15

BUSLOAD OF MISFITS

For a while after that, nothing happened. But once we were about a half hour down the road, I started hearing this leaky tire sound.

"Psst!...Psst!"

When I looked around, the girl across the aisle was staring at me. She seemed kind of pretty, in a pretty-scary kind of way. I'd never seen a kid that young with a real tattoo before, but she had this crazy snake around her arm. She had some muscles too. That snake looked like it could wrap around my neck and squeeze my head right off. I couldn't help but wonder how old she was when she got it in the first place. I bet her first words were telling the tattoo artist what color its eyes should be.

"I'm Carmen," she whispered. "What's your name?"

"Rafe," I whispered back.

"What'd you do?" she said.

"Huh?"

She looked at me like she'd just figured out how dumb I was. "Why are you here?" she said.

"Oh," I said. "I got expelled."

"Is that all? That's nothing. I once—" she said.

But then I heard a lion roar from the front of the bus.

"WHO'S TALKING???"

Fish was on his feet and coming up the aisle before I could even break a sweat. At least he wasn't looking at me.

"CARMEN, WAS THAT YOU JABBERING BACK HERE?" he said.

"Nah," she said, like she barely cared. "I heard someone, though."

"Yeah, I'll bet," Fish said, right in her face. Then he looked around at all of us. "Next one of you cockroaches to let out a peep gets ten extra pounds in their pack tomorrow morning! Are we clear? Do not test me on this."

Nobody answered. I guess we were all learning the rules of the game pretty fast. And we were all in the same boat.

Or on the same doomed bus, anyway.

But then that got me thinking.

This wasn't a program you signed up for on purpose. Everyone on that bus had done *something* to get themselves shipped out here for a week of suffering. Maybe something really bad.

What was Carmen about to say?

So if you were me, you know what else you'd be thinking, right? *What did all these other kids do?* And, *How far to the nearest hospital?*

Some of them seemed kind of sad and scared, but some of those kids just plain *looked* like their favorite hobby was ripping other people's faces off. (Hello, Carmen!) I know you're not supposed to judge a book by its cover and all that, but at the time, the cover was all I had to work with.

But that got me thinking about something else. What did everyone see when they looked back at me?

What did *my* cover look like?

FIRST TO DIE

THE RAFE KHATCHADORIAN STORY

Pweez Don't Hurt Me!

The Rafe Khatchadorian Story

Cloudy with No Chance of Survival

THE RAFE KHATCHADORIAN STORY

WELCOME TO CRAZYTOWN

The Rafe Khatchadorian Story

DON'T EVEN THINK ABOUT It

THE RAFE "BONE CRUSHER" KHATCHADORIAN STORY

Okay, I know I'm not exactly the type you run away from in a dark alley. But the point is, everyone on that bus was some kind of misfit, troublemaker, juvie, or whatever.

I don't know which one of those things I was. Maybe all of them. I didn't really like thinking about it.

And maybe it didn't matter anyway. At least on that bus. Because we were all cockroaches now.

CHAPTER 16

BASE CAMP BLUES

A ll right, cockroaches, listen up!" Fish said. "Welcome to Rocky Mountain High Base Camp. This is where your journey starts, and if you've got what it takes to make it through the week, this is where it'll end. Now grab your gear and follow me."

"What if we don't have what it takes?" someone said, making Carmen snort a laugh.

"Follow me anyway," Fish told us.

Base camp wasn't much. There were a couple of ancient buildings, but it didn't look like anybody lived in them. I saw some other groups too—mostly kids, and they all looked about as happy to be there as I was.

Pittman and Fish hustled us around the back

of the bus and handed out some old beat-up backpacks for us to put our stuff in.

"I suggest you bring only what you need," Sergeant Pittman said. "You'll be carrying those packs for the next week. Everything else will be here waiting for you."

Every pack came with a sleeping bag (mine smelled like a giant old sock), a climbing helmet (with someone's leftover hair inside, and what I swear looked like brain matter), and some of the supplies we'd use to make camp.

I jammed most of the stuff from my suitcase into the ratty backpack, since I hadn't brought much to start with. Just some clothes, an extra pair of shoes, my flashlight, my toothbrush, and my notebook with three pens in a big Ziploc bag. Besides the ban on electronics, we weren't allowed to bring any of our own food either. In fact, I didn't see any food at all, which seemed weird.

And a little scary.

After that, they marched us over to the main building for "orientation." Once we were all lined up there, some older guy in fatigues and a T-shirt came outside. Sergeant Pittman told us to sound off and give him our names, which meant I'd have another chance to learn some of the people I was about to be stranded with.

"Excellent! It's really great to meet you guys," the guy said. He flashed a big smile like he was in a toothpaste ad, but that didn't make me feel any better. I mean, what's the last thing you see on a shark before it eats you? A big mouthful of teeth, that's what.

"Good afternoon, boys and girls. I'm Captain Crowder, and I'm here to welcome you to The Program," he said. "You all have quite the adventure ahead. You might even have some fun this week."

There was some nervous laughter, until Fish told us all to "ZIP IT!"

Meanwhile, Captain Crowder was walking up and down like he was inspecting the troops. Which I guess he was.

"One goal of wilderness trekking is to leave the woods, mountains, rivers, and streams a little better than we find them," Crowder said. "That's exactly what your parents and guardians have asked us to do with you. By next Saturday, each of you will be better off than you are today. Maybe a lot better off."

"Sheesh. What is this, Wilderness and Feelings Camp?" Carmen whispered next to me. "Someone get me outta here."

"In the meantime, let me give you one piece of advice," Crowder told us. "You should think of The Program as a *team sport*. Believe me when I say you're going to need each other to get through this."

"I don't think so," Carmen said.

I didn't know *what* to think yet.

"And just like any team sport"—Crowder kept going—"there are rules to be followed. Break them, and you suffer. Follow the rules, and I guarantee you'll thrive here."

It was easy to see why Mrs. Stricker had picked this place for my trial. They were more rules-happy here than at HVMS. Maybe I could even introduce her to this Crowder guy. Then they could get married and live grumpily ever after, in a land far, far, far, far, far…FAR…away.

"So!" Captain Crowder said. "Now that we understand how this place works, any questions?"

Everyone kind of looked around at each other. I wasn't sure if it was another trap, or if we were allowed to talk now.

Finally, the musclehead kid, Arnie, spoke up.

"What's the deal on food?" he said. "'Cause I'm starving and I don't see any."

Captain Crowder laughed like that was a good one. "Excellent question," he said. "And in fact, what a perfect transition to your first obstacle. Sergeant Pittman? Sergeant Fish? You may take it from here."

"All right, people, let's move out," Pittman said. "Daylight's burning and we've got work to do."

"Enjoy!" Crowder told us as we headed off for whatever came next. "Oh, and, children? Have a wonderful time!"

He seemed like a decent old guy. He was all happy, and encouraging, and nothing like the Sergeants. So then…why didn't I trust him?

I guess it didn't matter. We were already on our way to our first "obstacle," and the way Fish and Pittman were marching us, I wasn't going to have a lot of time to think about Crowder—or his overly nice shark teeth.

CHAPTER 17

THE TOWER

What are we doing now?" I asked Pittman while we were marching through some woods and high grass up to my eyeballs. I could barely see where we were going, so I stuck close to the tall people.

"You'll see," Pittman said. "I think you're going to like it."

And since everything was kind of upside down here, I didn't know if she meant I was *actually* going to like it. All I knew about Pittman was that she was "nicer" than Fish. Which isn't the same thing as *nice*.

A minute later, we came out of the woods and into another big wide-open space.

"Ladies and gentlemen, welcome to the first of your nine obstacles for the week," Pittman said. "Also known as—the Tower."

For about thirty seconds there, I got kind of excited. Maybe Captain Crowder was right. Maybe I *was* going to have at least a little molecule of fun while I was here.

But then Pittman started explaining what we were actually doing here.

"Everyone take a look at that top platform," she said.

I looked up, but I couldn't see much.

"On that platform is a locked box," she said. "And in that box are your dinner rations for tonight."

"Okaaaay," Burp said, like he was expecting a big twist.

Veronica said something too, but you needed ultrasonic hearing to pick up anything from her.

"You'll have five minutes to get all eight of yourselves up there, grab those rations, and bring them back down to the ground," Pittman said. "That should be plenty of time—*if* you work as a team."

"And if not"—Sergeant Fish butted in—"well, there's always breakfast tomorrow."

"Nuh-uh!" Arnie said. "Are you, like, totally serious? I'm already starving!"

"One way to find out," Fish said. Which meant yes, they were about as serious as a case of poison ivy in your boxers.

In other words—if we didn't get it done, we didn't eat.

"Drop your packs, put your helmets on, and get ready to go," Pittman said. "You start in ten... nine...eight..."

I looked around at everyone while I was throwing on my helmet and trying to adjust the straps. They all looked about the same way I felt right then. Confused, nervous, but *mostly* hungry.

"...seven...six...five...four..."

I hadn't been on too many teams before, but none of them ever looked like this one. And I don't mean that in a good way. I was already wondering if we'd be snacking on our socks later. Hopefully not.

"...three...two...one...GO!" Pittman said, and we all took off running like our lives depended on it.

Which, if you believed our stomachs, they kind of did.

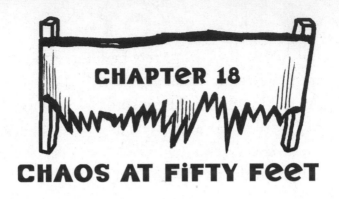

CHAPTER 18

CHAOS AT FiFTY FEET

I'm not bragging or anything, but I'm pretty fast on my feet, which comes with the territory of being chased around by so many bullies over the years. All eight of us went after that tower like it was made of chocolate cake, and I was the first one to get there.

That meant I was the first to start climbing one of the rope ladders at the bottom.

And *that* meant I was the first to face-plant right back into the dirt when my ladder flipped over. Those things were harder to climb than they looked. In fact, a few seconds later it was raining cockroaches.

"You've got to work together, people!" Sergeant

Pittman yelled at us. "You can't just run at this willy-nilly!"

My stomach felt emptier than a Diarrhea Fan Club meeting, and my dinner was sitting in a box about a hundred feet up. We had to keep moving, because there was no way I was lasting the night without some chow.

Arnie was the first to figure out that one person should hold each ladder steady while someone else climbed.

"You! Snake girl!" he said to Carmen. "Go!"

"Don't tell me what to do," Carmen said.

"I'll go," Thea said, and pushed right by her.

"And don't push me!" Carmen said.

"Do you want to argue, or do you want to eat tonight?" Sergeant Pittman said.

It took a while, but with Arnie holding the ladder, everyone finally made it up to the first platform. (Then Arnie climbed up with his astounding jock muscles.) But we still had two more levels to go, and then all three to come back down again.

"FOUR MINUTES LEFT!" Fish yelled.

The next climb was made out of tires, like one big wall of doughnuts (I wish!). I didn't know how we were *supposed* to do it. I just jumped on and kept going.

Which is why I got a sneaker to the head from Diego a second later.

"Watch it!" I said.

"YOU watch it!" he said.

"Just MOVE!" Burp yelled—right before he got a sneaker to the head from me. (I guess that's what the helmets were for.)

When I reached the top of those tires, Diego put out his hand.

"Here!" he said, and pulled me onto the next platform. Then I turned around and pulled Veronica up. I think she said thanks, but I couldn't hear her.

"There you go!" Pittman said. "Now you're thinking like a team!"

"THREE MINUTES!" Fish yelled. "MOVE, MOVE, MOVE, MOVE, MOOOOOVE!"

The next part was the most complicated. There were two big climbing ropes that went up through this whole spiderweb of nets and more ropes, and then a little opening you had to pass to reach the top platform. It might have all seemed pretty awesome if we hadn't had so much on the line.

But we did. So it didn't.

Carmen and Arnie got up to the platform first while everyone else struggled with the climb.

"Here's the box!" Carmen yelled. "Let's go!"

"Nobody comes down until EVERYONE gets to the top!" Pittman yelled. "You're not done yet!"

D.J. and I were the last ones still on those ropes, and he'd already left me in the dust. That meant I was bringing up the rear, which was bad enough. But then I looked down…

…down…

…down…

…all the way to the ground.

That's when everything went kerflooey.

I don't know what happened exactly. It was like a vacuum cleaner sucked the air right out of my lungs. My face got really hot, and all I could hear was this rushing sound like the inside of a seashell. It was like my stupid bad dream all over again.

"HURRY UP!" D.J. yelled.

"I AM HURRYING!" I yelled, even though I wasn't. Not anymore.

My terrible dream was all I could think about. My arms and legs were just cooked spaghetti by now, and all I could think was *Don't fall, don't fall, don't fall*….

By the time I finally got up to that

98

platform, I felt like I'd run a marathon. Backward. On one foot. And we weren't done yet.

"ONE MINUTE!" Fish yelled.

"We're never going to make it!" Arnie said.

"Yes we are! Let's go!" Thea said, and they practically threw that food box down to the middle platform as everyone started to climb down.

I didn't even care about eating anymore. All *I* wanted was a nice big piece of solid ground. And I guess that's what kept me going. The whole thing was a blur.

In fact, I barely even heard Sergeant Fish counting down the last seconds. People were yelling, and bodies were flying, and I was sweating my way through those tires again, looking longingly at the safe and solid ground, when he shouted out—

"THREE...TWO...ONE...GAME OVER, COCKROACHES! BETTER LUCK NEXT TIME!"

That seemed about right. It wasn't like our luck could get much worse, anyway.

Especially mine. Because this one was all on me. And everyone else knew it.

CHAPTER 19

TAG, YOU'RE IT

Well, that was pathetic!" Sergeant Fish said. "My great-grandma could have gotten farther than you cockroaches, and she's been dead for twenty years."

I was barely listening. I just lay there flat on my back, feeling like my lungs were two squashed watermelons. I could start to make out grumbles from the other kids. And I was thinking, *WHAT JUST HAPPENED?*

It's not like I was afraid of heights. Or at least, I didn't used to be. But as soon as I looked down from that tower, my brain turned into Jell-O.

Now Fish was yelling about how we'd all messed up, and everyone else was basically murdering me with their eyes. They didn't have much trouble getting down once they had the box. If I'd had a nickname in that place, it would have been Weak Link.

Sounds like the world's worst superhero, right? Yep, that's me.

"Well, the good news is, you made an effort," Sergeant Pittman told us. "And for that, you all earned your first tags. Good for you."

She held up something that looked like a bunch of shoelaces.

"What are those?" Burp said.

"Something to eat, I hope," Arnie said.

"Even better," Sergeant Fish told us. "You could survive all week out here without food. But these?" He and Pittman started passing them out. "These you can't live without."

Pittman handed me a string. It was just a piece of leather with one painted metal washer on it. My washer was orange. Thea's was green. Arnie's was white. I had no idea what the colors were for.

"By the end of day three—that's sundown on Tuesday—you need to earn *ten tags*. Not eight, and not nine-plus-a-good-effort. I mean *TEN TAGS*. Anything less than that sends you packing," Fish explained.

"WHAT?" I said, along with almost everyone else.

"But I have to finish!" D.J. said. "I go to juvie if I don't."

"Me too," Burp said. "I can't get kicked out."

"Well then, make sure you don't," Sergeant Pittman said. "And there's more. By the end of day six, you need to have earned *twenty* tags. Only those of you with twenty tags by sundown on Friday will be allowed to run the last day of this course. It's called the Ten, Twenty, and Out Rule."

Of course it is, I thought. *More rules. What a surprise.*

"You earn tags by running obstacles," Fish said. "You earn tags by doing your assigned work around camp. You earn them doing *unassigned* work too."

"And most of all, you earn tags by showing us you can be a team player on the trail," Pittman said.

"Dudes!" Diego said. "This is *so* not fair."

"Duly noted," Fish said.

And just like that, the hardest week of my life had just gotten harder.

Like, ten or twenty times harder, depending on how many days I lasted.

QUITTERS NEVER WIN
(BUT SINCE WHEN
AM I A WINNER?)

All right, gear up!" Sergeant Fish told us. "We still have some serious ground to cover."

Everyone was ticked off and grumbly about the new rule, their empty bellies, and me screwing up the Tower obstacle, but we started putting on our packs anyway.

Everyone except for Arnie.

"Hang on a sec," he said, crossing his arms. "Are we getting anything to eat or not?"

"Of course you are," Fish told him. "First thing tomorrow morning. In the meantime, you can chew on that poor performance of yours today."

"You've got to be kidding me!" Arnie said.

"I don't kid, kid," Fish told him.

"Oh yeah?" Arnie said, and sat back down. "Well, *I'm* not going anywhere until I get some food. How do you like that?"

For a second, nobody said a word. It was like one of those Old West movies where the saloon goes dead quiet. The piano stops playing. The poker players put down their marked cards. And every eye in the place lands on the one guy who's about to get a nice new hole in his skull.

But then Fish said the last thing I expected to hear.

"Maybe you should quit," he told Arnie in an eerily calm voice that was somehow scarier than his constant yelling.

"Say WHAT?" D.J. said.

"We're allowed to quit?" Thea asked.

"Sure you are," Pittman said. "The question is, can you afford to?"

"Well, Arnie? Can you?" Fish said. "Because there's plenty of food back at base camp. And I'm sure you can explain to your folks and everyone who signed you up for this why you lasted less than an hour out here."

Arnie was squinting back at Fish so hard, you couldn't even see his eyeballs. But then he just got up and started putting on his pack without saying a word. Fish had won.

"Yeah, I thought so," Fish said. "Now, let's get a move on!"

Meanwhile, my head was spinning in a whole new way. I was still back on the *quitting* thing.

After my big choke on the Tower, I figured I

had a zero percent chance of getting all the way through this thing. How was I supposed to climb a Rocky Mountain when I couldn't even climb a little tower without my brain going off-line?

Not to mention, none of these kids wanted me around anymore. I was Weak Link: Ruiner of Dinners. And if all the climbing, rafting, and starvation didn't kill me, that Ten, Twenty, and Out Rule definitely would.

In fact, the more I thought about it, the more it seemed like quitting wasn't just a *good* idea anymore. It was the *only* idea.

I could just see it now....

CHAPTER 21

LIFE O' CRIME

I QUIT!"

The words are out of my mouth before I can stop them. That's it—no turning back anymore.

Sergeants Fish and Pittman look at me like I'm scum, but everyone else cheers. They're planning the No-More-Weak-Link party.

Half an hour later, I'm sitting on my suitcase by the side of the road at Rocky Mountain High Base Camp, waiting for Mom to come pick me up. With any luck, I'll be eating cheeseburgers by sundown! Sure she'll be mad, but she'll get over it, right?

Except, that's when I hit my first glitch.

I wait for an hour.

Then two hours.

Five hours.

Fifteen.

After three days, I get the hint. Mom's not coming. This was my last chance to prove I could be a good son, and I blew it.

So I start walking. What choice do I have? I pick a direction, stick out my thumb, and hope for the best. Maybe someone will take pity on me, the lonely quitter.

Eighty miles later, someone does. A rusted-out pickup truck pulls over, and I hop in. I'm so tired, I don't even think about who might be behind the wheel.

Besides, how am I supposed to know he just escaped from prison or something?

My new friend's name is Rocco. It doesn't take long to find out he's a real desperado—but so am I now. That practically makes us family. We're going to stick together.

Next thing you know, I'm watching the parking lot for cops while Rocco knocks off an all-night convenience store...or two...or three. By the time the sun comes up, I've got fifty bucks in my pocket and a nasty case of brain freeze from all those slushees we stole. (I just can't resist that blue raspberry.)

Rocco and I make a good team, so we just keep going. The newspapers start calling us R&R, for Rocco and Rafe, but the cops can't pin us down. We're like ghosts. So we hop from state to state, and trade up to bigger jobs as we go.

Before you can say "I knew he'd turn out this way," there I am, wearing a Bugs Bunny mask and telling some lady at the First National Bank of Tucson to fill a bag with unmarked twenties.

It's our biggest job yet, but this can't go on forever. Rocco tells me we'd better split up and lie low until things cool off. It's for the best, he says.

I sure am going to miss him, though. He's like the incredibly dangerous, no-good older brother I never had.

After that, I head for the hills. I hike way up into the woods, scout out a decent hiding place, and settle in for the long haul. I could use the rest, anyway. This whole life of crime thing is exhausting. So I put my head down on a rock and close my eyes to take a quick nap....

Next thing I know, I'm waking up to the sound of choppers. It's the FBI! They're onto me! I can hear the tactical ground units moving into place too. Any minute now, they're going to have these woods surrounded.

Life in prison, here I come!

Tell Mom I love her. Tell Mrs. Stricker she was right all along. And tell Jeanne Galletta to go ahead and marry Whatshisname. I'm no good for her now. I guess it was just a matter of—

When I looked around, Sergeant Fish was spraying spittle in my face and everyone else was heading up the trail. I majorly zoned out on Planet Rafe this time.

"I'm all out of engraved invitations, Khatchadorian!" he said. "Are you coming, or what?"

"I'm coming!" I said. "I'm definitely coming." Then I hustled over to catch up with the group, the thought of Rocco fresh in my mind.

So much for quitting. I guess you can add that to the list of stuff I'm not very good at.

Besides, who can afford that life of crime?

CHAPTER 22

BURP

For our first hike, Fish put me on "point" at the head of the line. That meant if there was a thornbush to walk through, I was your guy. If there was a hole you might not see coming, just watch for my falling body. If there was a poison-dart frog waiting to attack (even though there are no poison-dart frogs in Colorado)—well, you get the idea. I was gonna get sacrificed first.

After a while, the trail got wider. That's when Burp started walking next to me.

"Hey," he said.

"Hey," I said.

"How's it going?"

"Okay," I said, because it was better than saying

I was having one of the four worst days of my life.

"By the way, don't worry about the Tower," Burp said. "And don't pay any attention to Fish either. That guy's all bark."

"Yeah, right," I said. "I'm pretty sure he has some bite in him too."

"Can you keep a secret?" Burp said, which was kind of weird. I was surprised he was talking to me at all. I didn't think anyone wanted my Weak Link stink getting on them. But Burp didn't seem like he cared.

"Yeah, I can keep a secret," I said. (Seriously, does anyone ever say *no* to that question?)

He walked a little closer then and looked at the ground when he talked. "Nobody's supposed to know this," he said, "but Sergeant Fish is actually my uncle."

"WHAT?" I said, and then said it again, but without shouting like an idiot. "*What?*"

"It's not like I get special treatment," Burp said. "I still have to call him Sergeant out here. But at home, he's Uncle Fish."

That was pretty hard to imagine. *Uncle Fish?*

What would that be like?

"So what are you doing in The Program?" I said. "Are you in trouble too?"

"Oh yeah. Big-time. Major trouble," Burp said.

"If I don't finish, I go to juvie for six months. Then after that, it's straight up to the big house."

This kid was barely making sense. "What big house?" I said.

"The state pen—hello? I'm talking about real prison," Burp said. "Once you're eighteen, that's where you go."

"You're *seventeen*?" I said. He looked younger than me. But Burp just shrugged. "What'd you do, anyway?" I asked.

"Mostly, it was an accident," he said. "I mean, I stole the car on purpose, sure. But I sure wasn't planning on driving through that bakery window. You should have seen the mess!"

"No way!" I said.

"Doughnuts all over the windshield. Frosting in the grill—"

"BURP!" Sergeant Pittman said. She was right behind us now, and I jumped about five feet. I swear, that ninja lady could walk through a pile of dead leaves without being heard.

"What did we say about the lying?" Pittman asked.

"I know, I know," Burp told her. "I was just goofing around."

"Well, cut it out!" she said.

After that, he just kept on walking up the trail like we'd been talking about the weather or something.

"So is anything you just said…you know—like, true?" I asked him.

"Not exactly," he said. "The truth is, I got expelled for throwing a whole box of cherry bombs down the school toilets—"

"BURP!" Pittman said.

"Okay, *one* cherry bomb," he said.

"Wow," I said, but maybe not for the reason he thought. I was starting to wonder how many flavors of crazy we had on this trip. These people were making me look downright normal, and that's saying something.

Still, I wasn't going to worry too much about Burp. He seemed pretty harmless to me. He wasn't a friend, exactly, but at least he wasn't an enemy.

And out there, I needed all the not-an-enemies I could get.

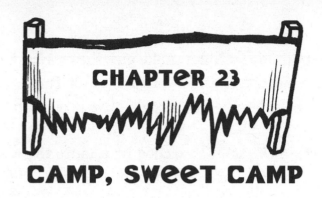

CHAPTER 23

CAMP, SWEET CAMP

When we got to our "camp," it looked pretty much identical to "woods" to me. There was a stream nearby, and some rocks on the ground where you could build a fire. And also there were trees. Lots and lots of trees.

"Camp, sweet camp," Sergeant Pittman said.

I think that was our rest break.

"All right, cockroaches. Packs off and let's get you divided into two teams," Fish said. "I need four volunteers for fire with Pittman, and four for shelter with me."

"I'LL DO FIRE!" everyone said at the same time.

"What a surprise," Fish said. "Diego, D.J., Thea, Burp. Come with me."

That put me with the snake girl, the cranky musclehead, and the one who didn't talk. But I guess it could have been worse. I could have been with Fish.

Sergeant Pittman marched us up into the woods to go peel birch bark and look for dry twigs and branches.

And of course, there were some more rules to hear about too.

"We work the buddy system out here," Pittman said. "Nobody goes anywhere alone. Ever."

"I got a question," Arnie said. "What if we have to go to the—"

"Come see me first," Pittman said. "And no making number twos until we show you how to dig a cat hole."

I was pretty sure I knew what she meant by "cat hole," but at the same time, I wanted no part of it. Some things are just meant to be flushed.

Speak for yourself!

"All right, everyone pick a buddy," Pittman said, and I felt a punch on my arm.

"Ow!" I said.

"Me and Rafe," Carmen said. "We got this."

"We do?" I said.

"All right, you two start on birch bark," Pittman told us. "Veronica and Arnie, you start with kindling. That's small twigs and other lighter materials. And remember, keep an eye on each other. If your buddy goes missing, it's on *you*."

"Do we get one of those tags for doing this?" Carmen said.

"Ask me when you're done," Pittman said. That probably meant yes, but not until we'd sweated a little. Or a lot. "Now, everyone get to work. I'll be right back. Shout out if there's a problem."

She picked up a log that was about as big as me and started carrying it back over to camp.

Exactly two seconds after Pittman was out of sight, Carmen started walking the other way.

"Where are you going?" I said, starting to follow her. "We're not supposed to split up."

She turned around and stared at me like you might look at an old lump of gum on the sidewalk.

"Oh, you're one of those," she said. "Always sweating about the rules?"

"No," I said. "That's one of my main problems. I'm

not. How do you think I got here in the first place?"

That made her smile. And her smile scared me just a little. Then she said, "You're kind of cute, you know that?"

Right before my jaw dropped down to the ground. If Carmen was trying to short-circuit my brain, it worked.

"I'll be back," she said. "I just got to talk to Veronica."

"Well…uh…yeah…uh…okay," I said.

Not that she needed my permission. She was already gone.

CHAPTER 24

JUST SO WE'RE CLEAR

Carmen was the exact opposite of Jeanne Galletta, except for one thing: I didn't have the first clue about how to act normal around her either.

Did this mean she liked me? Did I like her? Did it even matter what I thought?

When I saw Sergeant Pittman coming back through the woods, I waved over at Carmen to give her a heads-up. I didn't want her to get in trouble—and more important, I didn't want *me* to get in trouble either. But I couldn't even look at her when she came over from where Veronica was quietly collecting some twigs. I just kept peeling birch bark like it was the most important job in the world. Eyes on the job at hand.

"Is that all you two have gotten done?" Pittman said. "You're going to have to do better than that. Come on, double-time it."

"Sure thing, Sarge," Carmen said cheerily. "We're on it."

When I looked around again, I noticed that my pile of bark was about half the size it had been before. And Carmen's was a lot bigger. My bark was sitting right next to the snake girl like it had been there all along. She even took the big half.

After Pittman went over to check on Veronica and Arnie, Carmen gave me another one of those smiles. "Thanks for not saying anything," she said. "I'll get you back the next time."

"No problem," I said. "But you probably shouldn't go off like that again. I don't want either one of us to get in trouble."

Carmen looked over her shoulder to check on Pittman. Then she took a big step my way. She was close now—really close. That snake tattoo was practically hissing at me.

When she leaned in even farther, I got goose bumps on my goose bumps.

"Just so we're clear," Carmen said in this little whisper. "You may be cute, but I could put you in the hospital if I wanted to, and we both know it. So don't *ever* tell me what to do again."

Huh. Before she said all that, I actually thought Carmen was about to kiss me. Yes, I'm that dumb.

I mean, I've never kissed anyone. Not like that, anyway.

Honestly, I didn't know if I wanted her to do it or not, but it wasn't really up to me anyway. The only kiss I got that day was the kind you get from a snake.

And that's the kiss of death.

UP AND AT 'EM

I spent the rest of that night doodling in my "shelter," thinking about my empty stomach and whatever happened with Carmen. The campfire wasn't exactly the happiest place on earth, even though building it did earn us our second tags. So the next morning, when Sergeant Fish woke us up at the crispy crack of dawn, I *wanted* to be miserable about it.

But I just couldn't. I had one word running through my head, and that's all it took to eject me out of that tent like a piece of toast from a nuclear-powered toaster.

Okay, I didn't think I was waking up to blueberry pancakes and extra-crispy bacon, but

that didn't even matter. The point is, I was waking up to FOOOOOOD! BREAKFAST!

Back in the real world, what we woke up to was Sergeant Fish's morning breath, and not much else.

"Good morning, cockroaches!" he said. "Anyone hungry?"

"Anyone *not* hungry?" D.J. said.

"Well then, let's get right to it," Fish said, and my stomach started doing a happy dance all over again. "You're going to need some water for boiling," he told us.

"No problem," Burp said, and we started heading down to the stream.

"Hold on! We're going to need a fire for that water," Fish said.

"Okay," Thea said, and some of us broke off and turned back toward the fire circle.

"What—you think that fire burns itself?" Fish said. "You're going to need dry wood, and lots of it."

I was starting to get the idea about how much Fish liked messing with us. But that doesn't mean he was lying about all the work. I guess that's why we had to get up at a quarter past zero in the morning—so we could have breakfast sometime before lunch.

But we did it. We split up, peeled bark, gathered wood, started the fire, boiled some creek water, and even cooked the food ourselves, once Fish and Pittman told us how. And when we finally, finally got around to the eating part, it was just two scoops of the lumpiest, grayest, lukewarmest, most unbelievably delicious oatmeal I've ever had in my life.

You know how they say everything tastes better outdoors? Well, everything tastes even *better-er* when you're outdoors *and* all you've had for the last twenty-four hours is water, spit, and air.

And I don't even *like* oatmeal.

"I want you all to remember something," Pittman said while we were sucking down that glop. "Most kids who go to bed with empty stomachs don't know where their breakfast is coming from either. So keep that in mind the next time you *think* you're hungry."

Nobody said anything to that, unless "mmmm" and swallowing noises counted.

But I heard what Sergeant Pittman said. I definitely appreciated breakfast in a whole new way that day. In fact, I'd say it was just about the happiest twelve to fifteen seconds I'd had in a long, long time.

CHAPTER 26

MORE THAN ONE
WAY TO PLAY

As soon as we were done eating, D.J. got up and started collecting everyone's dirty dishes. I didn't think too much about it until Sergeant Pittman gave him a big smile.

"Thank you, D.J.," she said. "You can wash those down at the stream. And here's this too." Then she reached into her pocket and handed him a blue-painted metal washer. Another tag!

"Pay attention to D.J., roaches," Fish told us. "Taking on jobs without being asked is worth something around here. Don't think we forgot how many tags each of you still needs to pass this course."

I'd almost forgotten—this wasn't just a week of torture. It was a kind of game too. The kind you start losing as soon as you forget you're playing it.

I'd been sweating plenty about food, and Carmen, and Fish, and falling off a mountain, but if I didn't start worrying more about earning those tags, none of the rest would matter. I'd be out robbing banks with my good friend Rocco before you knew it.

In other words, I needed a strategy to get all of those tags. And the first thing I could think of was to talk to the kid who was playing the best game so far. So I picked up a couple of extra spoons lying around and carried them down to the stream where D.J. was washing up.

"You did that on purpose, right?" I asked, squatting next to him.

"Well...if you want to be nosy about it—yeah."

"It was a pretty good move," I told him. "You're the only one with three tags now, and all the rest of us still have two."

D.J. looked down at the string around his neck.

"Oh, that?" he said. "Yeah, that was cool too. But I just wanted the bowls."

"The bowls? What for?" I said.

"'Cause I'm still starving," he said. He took the first one off the stack and licked it all the way around the inside, burying his face in as far as he could.

"And *that's* what you call seconds!" he said, and reached for another.

D.J. did know how to play this—but just not in the way I thought.

"Go ahead if you want," he said, and pointed at the other bowls. "You can have three, but I get the other six, 'cause I thought of it."

GROWL

Well, this is a setback.

I looked into one of those bowls, and there were at least a couple of good-sized lumps still sitting there. My stomach whispered hello at them.

Besides, those lumps were food. Food was energy. Energy was what I needed to earn those tags. And like I said, those tags were what it was all about.

In other words—*strategy*.

"Well, maybe just a little taste," I said. And neither one of us headed back up to camp until every one of those breakfast dishes was sparkling clean.

After my talk with D.J., I decided it was time to put my game face on. I had to get organized.

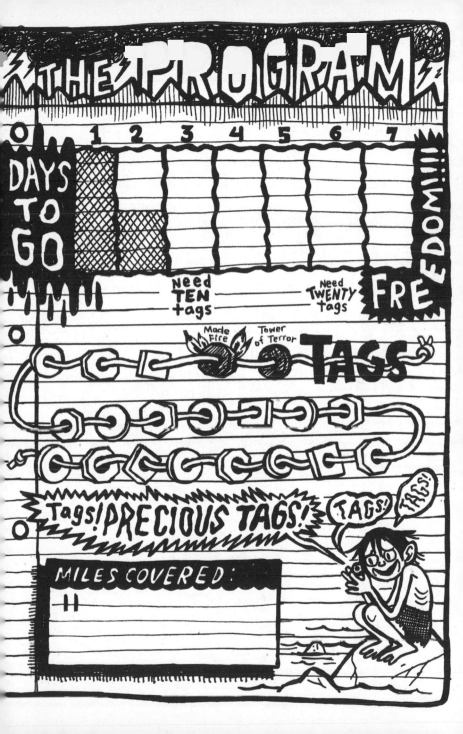

CHAPTER 27

BAD NEWS BUDS

Everyone circle up, shut up, and listen up," Fish said after breakfast. "It's time to think about hitting the mighty Arkansas River."

"Yes!" I said. I only kind of regretted it when I looked around and everyone was staring at me.

This was the one thing I was kind of looking forward to. White-water rafting sounded awesome to me. And I needed to show everyone that I could be something besides Weak Link.

There was only one thing missing for my grand plan.

"Where are the rafts?" I said.

Fish reached out with his pointer finger and toink-toinked me on the forehead. "Right in there," he said.

"Huh?"

"Welcome to obstacle number two, cockroaches. You're going to be figuring these rafts out and building them for yourselves."

"With *some* instruction," Pittman said. She was already drawing something in the dirt with a stick.

"We're going to need a donkey load of wood for this," Fish said. Which I guess made us the donkeys. "Me and Sergeant Pittman have already scoped out the area, and there should be enough usable wood here for two rafts. So pair up with your same buddy from yesterday and start working."

That meant me and Carmen. Again. She was already looking at me like I was some kind of after-breakfast snack.

So while everyone started getting ready, I went over to where Sergeant Pittman was packing up her gear.

"Sergeant Pittman, can I ask you something?" I said.

"I don't know—can you?" she said.

"I was just wondering, how long are we sticking with our buddies?" I said. "For the whole week, or—"

"Why? Is there a problem?" she said.

"Well…" I said.

"Yeah, Rafe, is there a problem?" someone else said behind me.

Gulp.

I turned around, and Carmen was standing right there with her arms crossed. She didn't say any more, but I could still hear her (and her snake friend) loud and clear: KEEP YOUR MOUTH SHUT OR I'M GOING TO PUT YOU IN THE CHOPPED MEAT SECTION.

And I was pretty sure she could too.

"No," I said. "No problem. Why would there be a problem? I was just, you know…curious."

"We done here?" Sergeant Pittman said, and I could feel the two of them looking at me from either side, like some kind of double whammy.

"I guess so," I said.

"Come on, Rafe," Carmen said. When she put an arm around my shoulder, I flinched. "We've got work to do," she said.

But you and I both know what she meant.

She meant *I* had work to do. Enough work for two.

CHAPTER 28

TROUBLE MAGNET

Anyone who's read my other books about my middle school "experience" probably knows a couple things about me:

1. I get into a little trouble once in a while.
2. Okay, a lot of trouble. More than once in a while.
3. Sometimes it's my own fault.
4. BUT SOMETIMES IT'S NOT!

And really, it's number four on that list that I don't get. You ever feel like you're walking through life with a big KICK ME sign on your back? I do. All the time. It's like I'm some kind of trouble magnet, and I can't do anything to stop it.

Like for instance, I knew exactly why I got stuck in The Program. That was (mostly) my own fault. But I had no idea why Carmen picked me as her own personal dartboard. She just did.

That's kind of the point.

Was I *afraid* of Carmen? Yes, I was. But that wasn't the main reason I kept my mouth shut in front of Sergeant Pittman.

I was doing whatever I had to do to earn those twenty tags and make it all the way to the finish line. In the meantime, I'd deal with what I had to deal with—especially Carmen.

Besides, it was only for a week. At Camp Wannamorra, I had to deal with Doolin and the Bobcats for over a month. And at HVMS, I had Miller the Killer making my life miserable for NINE months.

A week was nothing. I could put up with anything for that long.

At least, that's what I kept telling myself.

Over, and over, and over again.

CHAPTER 29

ALL THE WORK AND HALF OF THE CREDIT

We spent the next bunch of hours looking for fallen trees the right size...

...and pulling them all into a pile...

...and laying them out in rows...

...and getting crosspieces...

...and tying them together with knots that Pittman and Fish showed us...

...until it actually started to look like a couple of real live rafts.

And when I say "we," I mean everyone but Carmen. She spent most of her time telling me what to do, and what *not* to do, and looking busy whenever Pittman and Fish came around to inspect the rafts. All I know is, I never stopped moving.

Still, you can bet Carmen was first in line when Pittman started giving out that next round of tags.

"Good work, guys," she said. She handed me an orange washer, and Carmen got a purple one.

The real surprise came about a second later, when everyone else was starting to make lunch. That's when Fish clamped one of his big Fish hands on my shoulder.

"Let's take a walk," he said.

I didn't like the sound of that.

"What did I do?" I said. "Am I in trouble?"

"Not exactly. We just have to talk," he said, which isn't the kind of answer you want when someone like Fish is marching you off into the wilderness.

"Where are we going?" I said.

"Just keep walking," Fish told me.

The next thing I knew, we were heading up into the woods away from camp. Even worse, he was walking me away from Pittman and all the other kids. Also known as potential witnesses to whatever horrible punishment was coming my way.

And all I could think now was—*Uh-oh. Dead kid walking.*

CHAPTER 30

FISH TALK

As soon as we were out of earshot of everyone else, Fish got right to it.

"Let me ask you a question," he said. "Do you have a crush on that girl?"

I don't know what I was expecting him to ask, but that wasn't it. And since I didn't have a good answer, I tried stalling him a little.

"What girl?" I said.

"*Cockroach...*" Fish said, which sounded a lot like *We can do this the easy way or we can do this the hard way*. I knew who Fish was talking about, and he knew I knew it.

"Oh? Carmen? No, sir," I said, with my best innocent face. "No crush there."

"Then why are you picking up the slack for her all the time?" Fish said.

"Huh?" I said. This whole thing kept changing faster than I could keep up. "Hang on. You know about all that?"

"It's kind of hard to miss," Fish said.

"So then why are you letting her get away with it?" I asked him.

Fish reached over and toink-toinked me on the forehead again. "You don't get it, do you?" he said. "This isn't middle school, kid, and I'm not your homeroom teacher. Out here, you live with your own choices. You want to walk around with someone else's footprints on your back? That's up to you."

Uh…

This is the part where I reach into my pocket and pull out one of my Official Free Passes. It's like a Get Out of Jail Free card. I hand it over to Fish, he lets me walk away, and we both forget this conversation ever happened. Yeah, in my dreams!

And since *that* wasn't an option, I tried one of the oldest tricks in the book. *Changing the subject.*

Dear _____,
        Name of adult
This conversation is
now over. Thank you
and have a nice day.

May be applied to any question,
including but not limited to: What
were you thinking? Who made this
mess? Who do you think you are?
What do you have to say for yourself? And So! Much! More!

It doesn't always work, but it's always worth a shot.

"Shouldn't we be getting back?" I said, trying to be as smooth as possible. "I'll bet they have those rafts on the river by now."

And guess what? It worked! Fish actually cracked a real smile and everything.

"You think that dinky little stream back there is the mighty Arkansas River?" he said.

"It's not?" I said.

"Come here," Fish told me.

Instead of heading toward camp, we started going deeper into the woods. After a minute, Fish ducked us under a bunch of pine branches, and we came out onto this big open piece of rock.

"Now *that's* what you call a river," Fish said.

And all I could say was…

I took a step back from that edge and tried not to look down.

"So then, why did we build the rafts in the woods?" I said. "Why didn't we do it down there?"

But I was learning quick, and I was pretty sure I already knew the answer.

"That would have been too easy," Fish told me. "Plus, the wood we needed wasn't by the river. And by the way," he said, "changing the subject doesn't change the fact that you've got some thinking to do. Understand?"

"Yeah, I understand," I told him. What else was I going to say?

"Good," Fish said. "Now let's go, cockroach—back to camp! Time for your next obstacle. Move, move, move, move, MOOOOOOVE!"

CHAPTER 31

A (VERY) QUICK DIP

The next obstacle was kind of like the way Pittman described the whole program. It wasn't that complicated. All we had to do was take our new rafts and bring them down a path to the river. But it wasn't easy either. That trail was S-T-E-E-P. And those rafts were H-E-A-V-Y. By the time we carried them all the way down to the mighty Arkansas, I'd sweated a whole river of my own.

But at least I got another tag out of it. That, and the one I got for digging latrines, put me at five—halfway to the ten I needed before sunset the next day. Not too shabby. It finally felt like things were looking up.

For about a minute, anyway.

The place we came to was called a *put-in*, because that's where people PUT their rafts IN the water. (I guess raft people don't have much imagination.) There was a parking lot with a couple of trucks, some trailers with kayaks on them, and a big storage locker with life vests, wet suits, paddles, and I don't know what else.

Even though you could see some rapids way downstream, the water by the put-in was calm, like a swimming hole. "Can we jump in?" I asked Pittman.

"If you want to," she said. "But that river's pretty cold."

"Sounds good to me," Arnie said. We already had our shoes off, and everyone headed right for the water. "Last one in is a rotten—"

In case you were wondering, that was the sound of eight kids screaming all at the same time.

When Pittman said the water was *cold*, I thought she meant it was just *regular* cold. Like coming-out-of-your-faucet cold or nice-cool-drink-of-water cold.

How was I supposed to know she meant eighty-below-zero, turn-you-into-an-ice-cube, hurts-just-to-touch-it, deadly-freezing-*frozen* cold? That water was chillier than Mrs. Stricker's heart sitting on top of the North Pole on a cloudy day. Another half degree colder, and we would have been there for skating instead of rafting.

Let's just say it was the world's shortest swim.

By the time we got back on dry land, all you could hear was chattering teeth.

"We're s-s-s-supposed to go r-r-r-RAFTING in th-th-that?" Diego said.

"Technically speaking, you'll be rafting *on* the river, not in it," Pittman said. "Besides, that's what the wet suits are for."

"How about dry suits? You got any of those?" Burp said.

"My hands are blue!" Thea said.

"I can't feel my lips!" D.J. said.

"Enough with the bellyaching!" Fish said. "Just give it a little time. Trust me, cockroaches, you'll get used to it."

I don't think he meant the water, though. I'm pretty sure he meant the pain and suffering.

But either way, I wasn't so sure I believed him.

CHAPTER 32

RIVER SCHOOL

For the rest of the afternoon, we had something called river school. If you've never heard of it before, don't worry. Neither had I. All you need to know is that it's one of the top five most boring things I've ever done.

Fish talked (and talked) to us about hydrology, ecology, biology, and more *ologies* than I can remember. I think there were a couple of *ographies* in there too.

We also learned about safety, safety, and more safety. After another raft inspection, Pittman made it sound like there were at least thirty-three different ways to ruin your life by not paddling correctly or "staying sharp on the river."

They told us what eddies and wave trains were too. And supposedly, it was super-important for us to know every last difference between Class 1, 2, 3, 4, and 5 rapids. They went over it about six times.

Finally, they put us up on the rafts. *On dry land.* That's where we learned to paddle. (Kind of.) I think everyone was getting as bored as I was by then.

"If you fall off, float on your back and keep your feet in front of you," Pittman said.

"Don't try to fight the water!" Fish said about a dozen times. "The water always wins."

"And remember," Pittman told us, "you *always* work as a team. Any questions?"

"Yeah," Arnie said. "What's for dinner?"

Pittman ignored him. "Okay then," she said. "That means we can move on to the quiz."

"Say *what*?" Diego said. "Nobody said anything about a quiz."

"Duly noted," Fish said. He and Pittman were already busting out the paper and pencils.

"Anyone who gets at least eight out of ten questions right on the first try earns an extra tag,"

Pittman said. "Less than that, and you take the quiz again—after a one-hour review session."

In other words, I've never wanted to pass a quiz so much in my life.

And here's another surprise for you. I didn't get eight out of ten answers right. I got *nine* out of ten! So I guess I was paying a little more attention than I thought. Maybe because I was a little more scared of this rafting than I was letting on. Heck, if I could *die* because I didn't know when the Revolutionary War started, I bet I'd do better on history quizzes.

Carmen passed the quiz too. In fact, her answers were all exactly the same as mine.

Imagine that.

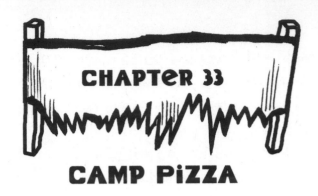

CHAPTER 33

CAMP PiZZA

When Fish said we were having something called camp pizza for dinner that night, I got pretty excited. We all did.

But if you're thinking, *Don't get your hopes up, Rafe*, then you're one step ahead of me. I had to find out the hard way.

Camp pizza is made of saltines and tomato soup. You dip the saltines in the soup, and when you eat it, you say, "Mmm, pizza."

Yeah, *right*. Camp pizza tastes like pizza the way licking a cow might taste like a hamburger.

I didn't even care. I just wanted get inside my sleeping bag, stick my head on a balled-up T-shirt for a pillow, and go to sleep for the next eighty-two hours. I think Thea was already asleep in her soup. And Burp looked like he'd been awake since he was born.

"I'm ready to pass out right now," D.J. said. "Food or no food."

"I hear that," Carmen said, because I guess she was so tired from all that goofing off.

"Paddles in at oh seven hundred, people," Pittman said. "That means wet suits on at six thirty and chow at six." Which *really* meant we had to get up at five if we wanted to make breakfast in time.

But meanwhile, all I had to do was sleep. I didn't have to build anything, carry anything, learn anything, or even listen to anyone until the sun came up again. The ground under my sleeping bag may have been hard and lumpy, but after that long day we'd had, it felt like I was checking into the MegaLuxe Hotel.

And I thought, *Ahhhh! Best part of the day!*

And then it was more like *zzzzzz*…because I was out like a broken headlight.

Right up until the world's biggest thunderstorm came to town.

CHAPTER 34

STORM OF THE CENTURY

So imagine you're in your own bed at home. It's raining outside—hard. You can hear it falling on the roof and blowing against your windows. But you don't care. You're all wrapped up tight like a burrito, warm and dry in your blankets.

Okay, now take away the cozy part. And the warm, dry part too. While you're at it, put some holes in the roof and rip out the windows. In fact, take away everything except the rain, wind, thunder, and lightning.

Now throw in a flimsy tarp that makes Swiss cheese look like reinforced steel, and you'll have a pretty good idea of what it was like inside our shelter that night.

We were all shoved into the corners, trying to stay out of the drip-drip-drip-drips that kept coming in. Except then the drips turned into drops, and the drops turned into a waterfall. Most of our packs and bags ended up soaked.

I tried to pull my sleeping bag over my head, but that didn't get me too far. It wasn't like I was going to sleep, anyway. Not with all that lightning and thunder going off.

Every time we got a flash, I could hear Arnie counting on the other side of the shelter. It was like—

FLASH!

"One Mississippi, two Mississippi, three Mississippi, four Mississippi, five Mississippi, six Mississippi—"

And then—

KA-BLAM!

"What are you doing?" I said.

"Counting the miles," he said. "Every second is one mile. That's how far away the lightning is."

"So it's still, like, six miles away?" Diego said.

"Something like that," Arnie said.

"My dad got struck by lightning once," Burp said. "It was on a night just like this—"

"Shut it, Burp!" D.J. said. I guess Burp's reputation had gotten around camp by then. But Burp wasn't one of my problems that night. Everything else was.

And then—

FLASH!

We all counted this time. "One Mississippi, two Mississippi, three Mississippi, four Miss—"

KA-BLAM!

"Four miles," Diego said.

"Oh, man," D.J. said. "That's not good."

I could hear someone crying over in the girls' shelter, but I couldn't tell who it was. I think Sergeant Pittman was in there too, trying to calm them down. But I didn't get to figure it out because the next time around, it went like this—

FLASH! **KA-BLAM!**

And then two and a half Mississippis later, we had enough. We all bailed on our wet, miserable little shelter and made a beeline for the warm, dry tent that Fish had set up for himself.

"What are you people doing in here?" Sergeant Fish yelled at us. "It's just a little rain!"

"Yeah, and the Grand Canyon's just a little hole in the ground," D.J. said. "I think I saw that Noah guy going by in his ark."

"It's crazy out there!" I said.

"And we're scared!" Diego said.

"Oh, you're *scared*?" Fish said. "Well, why didn't you say so? Maybe we should all head over to the nearest IHOP for some pancakes until this blows over."

"Can we really do that?" Burp said, a little too excitedly.

"NO, WE CAN'T REALLY DO THAT! NOW GET OUT THERE, SECURE YOUR SHELTER, AND HUNKER DOWN!!!"

"But our shelter's toast!" Arnie said.

"Duly noted," Fish said. "I guess that means you'll have to tie it down properly this time."

"But—" I said.

"Now, go! MOVE, COCKROACHES!"

"But—" D.J. said.

"MOVE, MOVE, MOOOOOVE!!!!"

I didn't think anything could be scarier and louder than that storm, but I was wrong. So we all piled out of Fish's tent like five blind mice, and started looking for our flashlights, some rope, and whatever was left of our shelter.

Three words: Worst. Night. Ever. At least, until the next night.

CHAPTER 35

RAFE ON A RAFT

In the morning, the river looked about three times as high and five times as mean as the day before.

First thing after what passed for breakfast (soggy granola), we had to put on our wet suits. Which were already wet from the storm.

Have you ever put on a wet wet suit? It's kind of like trying to climb inside a tube of toothpaste. And then once you finally get it on, you try not to panic because it feels like there's no way you're ever getting that thing off again.

That's usually right about the time you figure out that you should have gone to the bathroom first.

When we got down to the river's edge, Pittman

and Fish were tying our two four-person rafts together into one big raft and putting all of our packs into two of those kayaks.

"Change of plans, people," Fish said. "The water's a little high this morning, so you'll head downriver as one team to make sure everyone sticks together."

"Why? Is the river more dangerous now?" Burp asked.

Fish and Pittman looked at each other, and then Pittman looked at Burp.

"It's fine, no problem at all," Pittman said, but that pause was just long enough for everyone to figure out the *real* answer. "Everyone gear up and let's shove off."

Nobody talked too much while we were putting on our life jackets and helmets. Then we picked up our paddles and piled onto that big raft.

"Remember everything we told you!" Pittman said. "I'll be out front in one kayak, and Sergeant Fish will come behind."

"Out there on the river, we talk and you listen," Fish said. "We call a command and you do it, no questions asked. That's how you—"

"Stay alive?" Carmen said.

"*Run a smooth expedition*," Fish said. "Now, let's do this! Move! Into the water!"

Pittman was out in the water by now, paddling in her kayak, while Fish shoved us off from the shore. I don't really know what he was expecting, but I'm pretty sure the next ten seconds didn't go the way they were supposed to.

As soon as he let go of the raft, we took off—*quick*. We flew right past Sergeant Pittman, who had way better control of her kayak than us newbies on our big raft, and just kept on going. Next thing I knew, we were shooting straight down the mighty Arkansas at top speed, like something out of a movie.

And if it *was* a movie, it would be called—

CHAPTER 36

RUNNING THE GAUNTLET

I can't tell you a whole lot about those first ten seconds. All I remember is the screaming.

"Something's wroooooong!" Thea yelled.

"You THINK?" Carmen yelled back.

"Where's Pittman and Fish?" Diego said.

I looked back and they were already about a mile behind us.

"SLOW DOWN!" Fish screamed.

"Verrrrrrrrry funnnnnnnnnnnny-y-y-y!" Thea yelled.

"How?!" the rest of us chimed in.

Pretty quick, the water went from fast to faster and white to whiter. We were up to our eyeballs in rapids before Fish and Pittman were anywhere near catching up to us. It didn't seem to matter how hard they paddled, they just couldn't make up the distance.

The rapids were like a roller coaster on steroids. We rode up the front of one wave, and—*slam!* Down on the other side. Up the next swell, and—*sploosh!* Back down again. That raft was bucking like a bronco, and all we could do was hold tight. Paddling? Forget about that. We were just trying to stay on.

We flew up—and down. And sideways. And around. And back up—and back down.

And here's the thing. I don't know exactly how long that part went on, but somewhere along the way, it actually started to get—fun. Sure, we were cold and wet and terrified, but at a certain point, we were also realizing something.

We weren't *just* screaming and out of control. We were actually *riding* those rapids!

It was awesome!

And dangerous!

And then…

That's when I saw what Fish and Pittman later called the Gauntlet, dead ahead. Emphasis on the *dead*.

When we came around the next bend in the river, we were headed straight at this WALL of white water. And just past the wall, there was another wall, and another. It looked like the whole river was standing up.

"I don't like…the look…of that!" Arnie said.

"Me neither!" I said.

"What are we going to do? What are we going to *do*?!" Carmen said.

"What CAN we do?" Thea said.

"EVERYONE HOLD ON!" I said.

"Hey!" Burp said. "This is just like the time when I—"

"SHUT UP, BURP!" everyone yelled—right before we hit that first wall.

All of a sudden, that raft wasn't underneath me anymore. It was more like in front of me. The whole thing stood up straight and we slid off like fried eggs off the grill at Swifty's Diner.

I tried to remember what Pittman and Fish had said about falling in. I put my feet out in front of me—at least I remembered that much—and my life vest kept me from going under. Mostly, though, my thoughts were going something like *glub-blug-blah-blab-glub-HELP!-blah-blub-glug....*

I wasn't *on* the raft anymore. Now I *was* the raft. We all were. When I looked around, I saw a bunch of helmets and life vests—but I couldn't tell who was who. It was just a big mess of cockroach soup, shooting downstream toward the calmer part of the river.

The good part about how fast the Gauntlet runs is that it doesn't take long to get spit back out of it. Pretty soon we were all stumbling up onto the banks and counting heads. We were soaking and bruised and a little shaken up, but we had ridden the rapids. If Pittman and Fish would have let us, I think some of us would have gone again. Myself included.

The Sergeants showed up pretty quick, anyway. Pittman looked scared, but Fish just looked mad. Maybe at the river. Maybe at himself for not catching up. Or maybe at us for not being superheroes.

"Everyone okay?" Pittman said.

"We're okay," Arnie said.

And in a weird way—I don't know if anyone else felt it—I actually felt like we were *more* than okay. We'd survived! And that's not all.

My hands were blue. I was shivering like a leaf in the wind. But more than anything, I was wondering how many tags we were going to get for this.

That's right—it was all about the game for me. *Still*.

And *that's* when I knew for sure that I was in it to win it.

CHAPTER 37

TAKING OUT THE TRASH

After that, Pittman towed Fish's kayak behind hers, and Fish took the raft with us.

I'm not going to lie. Fish was amazing on the river. He got us paddling all together, and we shot those rapids like fish in a barrel. It was capital AWE, capital SOME. I didn't fear for my life once.

But when we got to the take-out (where you TAKE your rafts OUT of the water, another example of clever raft naming), it was back to the same old Fish.

"All right, cockroaches, let's get you good-for-nothings doing some good for *something*. Everyone take a garbage bag," he said. Then he started handing bags out from this shed where we turned in our paddles and life jackets.

At the take-out, there was a parking lot, a picnic area, and some bathrooms, all with overflowing garbage cans. It looked like everyone who came there had the world's worst aim with their trash. Now it was up to us to "leave the place better than we found it," like Captain Crowder had said what seemed like ages ago.

"I want to see full bags, people," Pittman said. "A full bag earns a new tag! No slacking!"

I got busy right away. The end of day three was coming up fast, and I still only had nine tags, even after earning an extra by helping out with the cooking. I was right about our trip on the river being worth a little extra tag-wise, but I still had to hustle if I wanted to fill two garbage bags before sundown.

That's right, two bags. You haven't forgotten about Carmen, have you?

As usual, she spent most of her time *not* getting anything done while I did all the work. And to tell you the embarrassing truth, I didn't even think about it anymore.

But then I started to notice how quiet Carmen

was. That was weird—for Carmen. She wasn't even standing near anyone, and the only time she said anything was when some guy at the picnic area laughed at her tattoo. *Then* she said plenty, but I'm not allowed to put those kinds of words into this book.

Still, I could tell something was wrong. In fact, she hadn't bossed me around for hours, ever since our raft tipped over. I was starting to think maybe the mighty Arkansas had scared her more than she was letting on.

"You okay?" I asked her, once I'd made sure that everyone else was out of earshot.

"I will be soon," she said.

"What does that mean?"

"I mean, I'm out of here," she said. "I'm quitting this stupid program."

"*What?*" I said. That wasn't what I expected. At all.

"You heard me," she said. "Pittman and Fish can shove it."

"But you can't quit now," I said.

TIME OUT FOR A SECOND!

I know what you're thinking. Carmen quitting The Program could have been like Christmas, Thanksgiving, and my birthday, all rolled into one. Why would I ever say something as stupid as that?

There were a million things I could have said instead. And a million more I *should* have said.

Here's the thing. I don't think our rafting trip was the only part that scared Carmen. In fact, I'm pretty sure I'd just figured out who was the one crying in the girls' tent during that thunderstorm. I don't know—if I can be afraid of heights, maybe Carmen had a thing about water. Or maybe The Program was just getting to her.

And now I felt just a little, teeny, tiny bit sorry for her.

"Just finish out today," I said. "Get your tenth tag and then see what happens tomorrow."

"DON'T TELL ME WHAT TO DO!" she said.

"I'm not," I told her, because I could see a little of the old Carmen, and I wanted to keep my face arranged the way it was. "I'm just asking, what happens to you if you don't finish?"

For a while, Carmen didn't say anything to that.

I don't know what she was thinking, but that's pretty normal with her. Then finally, she kind of nodded.

"Yeah, okay," she said. "I'll give it another shot. But if I regret this, I'm going to quit, and then I'm going to kill you."

"Uh…" I said—right before she took that full garbage bag out of my hand, gave me her empty one, and started walking over to where Pittman was handing out the tags.

I never even got to say "You're welcome." So I guess Carmen and I were back to normal. For better or worse.

And speaking of worse, that's when I saw Sergeant Fish watching us from across the parking lot. He'd seen the whole thing. Now he just shook his head and walked away.

If he'd heard what we were talking about, he would have known I was being a *team player*. Maybe he'd even have given me an extra tag. But no. As far as Fish was concerned, I had a permanent set of Carmen-sized footprints all over my back.

Which maybe I did, and maybe I didn't.

But I couldn't worry about that. The sun was going down quick. I needed to be thinking about one thing, and one thing only.

Well, two things, I guess.

Strategy. And garbage.

CHAPTER 38

GOOD NEWS, BAD NEWS, WORSE NEWS

The good news was, I earned that tenth tag by sundown. Sure, it was a lot of garbage, and by the time I finished my second bag most of the other kids had already filled theirs. When I handed my bag to Fish, slightly lighter than the others, he gave me that look again and shook his head.

But that didn't matter. I had my tenth tag in my hand! That meant I got to keep going!

So did Carmen, Burp, Diego, Thea, Veronica, and D.J.

See? Check out my new flashy and updated report on The Program:

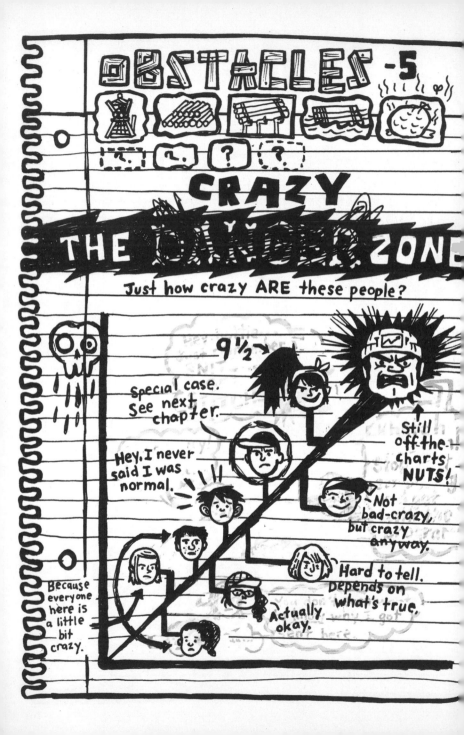

But you might have noticed my little note next to Arnie. That's the bad news.

I don't know how Arnie messed it up. All I know is that before we left that parking lot, Sergeant Pittman pulled out a walkie-talkie and radioed back to base camp. (I guess no one told her about that NO ELECTRONICS rule.) Then a little while later, Captain Crowder showed up in the world's oldest jeep to pick Arnie up and take him back.

It wasn't like I liked Arnie that much. He was nice enough, sure, but we'd never really talked for a long time. But still, I felt bad for him. I think everyone did.

"This isn't fair!" Thea said. "We've all been working hard!"

"Some of you have been working harder than others," Pittman said. "Arnie only had eight tags."

"And anyone who thought we were kidding about that Ten, Twenty, and Out Rule is sadly mistaken," Fish said.

That much was obvious. Because just like that, Arnie was O-U-T.

Since nothing ever stopped out there, we still

had to make a fire, build our shelters, cook some slop, and start thinking about our next ten tags.

Which brings me from the bad news…to the even worse news.

"What are we doing tomorrow?" Burp asked while we were all sitting around the fire later. "What's the next obstacle?"

Pittman pointed up. "That is," she said.

It was dark out, but when I turned around, I could see the cliffs in the moonlight, sticking up higher than the trees around us.

"Say hello to Devil's Highway," Fish said.

"Are we *climbing* that?" D.J. said.

"Sure are," Pittman said.

"Cool!" D.J. said.

I might have thought it was cool too—like maybe a week earlier. You know, before my whole panic-attack, brain-melt, Weak-Link situation on the climbing tower.

And those cliffs made that tower look like a step stool. The idea of climbing anything right now, much less something called Devil's Highway, made me want to throw up my teeny-tiny dinner.

Still, I knew I had to give this a shot. If I didn't, I was going be bunking with Arnie back at base camp. Mom was going to be majorly disappointed in me. Stricker and Stonecase were going to have a huge *Told-You-So* party. My little sister was going to finish middle school before I did. And the past three days of torture-on-the-trail were going to be for nothing.

Less than nothing, in fact. I'd be worse off than when I started.

"All right, time for some shut-eye," Fish said. "I want you all well rested and sharp for this climb."

Yeah, I thought. *Sharp. Like jagged rocks.*

I realized I probably wouldn't be getting much sleep after all.

CHAPTER 39

(UN)PLEASANT DREAMS

Greetings from ten thousand feet!

The whole world has tuned in to watch me make this climb. There are satellites and cameras everywhere, and the crowd down below stretches all the way to Utah. I've got about eight billion eyes on me as I ascend this vertical cliff face like the boss that I am.

I don't know what I was so afraid of. The way my hands and feet cling to the rock, even Spider-Man's jealous. I'm like one big piece of double-stick tape.

"Way to go, Khatchadorian!" I hear from the crowd. Is that Sergeant Fish down there? And I'm pretty sure Jeanne Galletta's sitting in front of her TV back at home, watching me and thinking, "Jared *who*?"

I stop just long enough to take an energy bar from the falcon that was trained to bring me snacks, since no one else has the nerve to climb this high. For a few seconds, I hang on with my toes while I scarf down the bar for a quick boost (not that I need it). Then I turn my attention to the last thirty yards of this climb.

This is it. The trickiest part yet. Somehow, I have to make my way under, over, and around this shelf of rock before I can stand at the top and take in the view. No problem, though. I grab a handhold, swing my legs around, execute a perfect twisting flip—

"OIIIIIIIH!" the crowd screams as I fly through the air. And then "AHHHH!" as my fingers lock on to the ledge at the very tippy-top of this mountain. All I have to do now is flex my freakishly large biceps and pull myself up onto flat ground. But then—

"Well, well, well," someone says. "Look who it is."

"That was impressive," another voice says. "Too bad it was all for nothing."

I look up, still hanging there by my fingers. And that's when I come face-to-face (-to-face) with the Petaluma Sisterhood, Ida P. Stricker and Charlotte P. Stonecase.

"Let me up!" I yell.

"Not so fast," Stricker says. "Did you finish your math?"

"What math?" I say.

"Or your book report?" Stonecase says.

"What report?" I say. "What book?"

"He didn't do his homework," Stonecase says, grinning like a goblin.

"He never did," Stricker says, and they both laugh so loud, it echoes off the Rocky Mountains.

Then they kneel down and start peeling my fingers off the edge of that cliff, one after the other.

"This little cockroach went to market," Stricker says.

"Stop it!" I yell.

"This little cockroach stayed home," Stonecase says.

"I'm going to fall!" I tell them desperately.

"This little cockroach had roast beef—"

"No I didn't! Not even close!"

"—and this little cockroach had none."

"HELP!" I scream. I'm dangling by one pointer, a pinkie, and two thumbs by now. But not for long.

"And this little cockroach went, 'Wee, wee, wee,' all the way home."

Pointer! Pinkie! Thumb! Thumb! One by

one, they rip my fingers off my perfectly chosen handhold.

"AUUUUUGHHHHHHH!!!!" I say.

I'm falling…falling…falling back to earth, and the last thing I hear before I hit the ground is Mrs. Stricker's voice.

"Oh, and one more thing," she yells after me…

CHAPTER 40

DON'T LOOK NOW

GOOD MORNING, COCKROACHES!"

"Hurhhh?" I said.

When I woke up, I was all twisted around in my smelly old sleeping bag. It was like waking up inside a cotton ball soaked in sweat.

"What time is it?" I said, trying to untangle myself.

"Time to mow down another challenge," Fish said. "Let's go! Move, move, move, move, mooooooove!"

Oh...man. I either needed to figure out how to stop dreaming, or just stop sleeping. I couldn't take too many more nightmares like that one.

Not to mention the day-mare that hadn't quite started yet.

I barely even remember the next part. I guess we had breakfast and hiked up to the base of Devil's Highway, then put on some harnesses and sat through climbing school. All I know is that it seemed like five minutes later when Pittman was saying, "Okay, who's first?"

And then Carmen's hand was clamping down on my shoulder.

"We got this," she said.

It was another buddy challenge. We were doing something called top-roping, where they had ropes already set on the cliff—two of them, side by side. Sergeant Fish and Sergeant Pittman were the *belayers*, which meant they held the rope at the bottom and kept an eye out for you. There was even a thing on the line they could use like brakes, anytime you slipped up. So supposedly, there was no risk at all.

I mean, unless your climbing rope broke.

Or your harness broke.

Or one of those little thin carabiner clippy things broke.

Or a big chunk of rock came loose and crushed your head on the way down.

Or if your belayer stopped paying attention, even for a second, maybe because they were distracted by one of the other seven kids they were supposed to be keeping track of.

But hey, other than that I felt perfectly safe.

"All right, here we go," Pittman said. She was Carmen's belayer and Fish was mine. "Look for a handhold, pull yourself up, and start climbing."

That part wasn't the problem. I mean, I know how to climb stuff. For me, it wasn't about *getting* up that cliff. It was all about *being* up there.

So as soon as I was about an inch off the ground, I just started thinking the same three words over and over.

Don't. Look. Down.

It was my strategy for this obstacle. That was exactly when everything went all screwy on the climbing tower. The second I looked down from that thing, my brain started to melt and I felt like I was going to explode into a million pieces.

So now I didn't care what it took. If I didn't look down, I couldn't know how high I was. And if I didn't know how high I was, I couldn't be afraid of heights. Right? That was the idea, anyway.

It really helped too. I mean, until it didn't.

After that, everything went really, really bad, really, really fast.

CHAPTER 41

KERFLOOEY, PART TWO-EY

So there I was, climbing and not looking down, climbing and not looking down, climbing and not looking down. It seemed like it was going okay, right up until—

"KHATCHADORIAN, WHAT ARE YOU DOING?"

Sergeant Fish was yelling at me.

"You're getting in your partner's way!" Fish said. "Watch out for Carmen!"

When I looked over (*not* down), she was right in my face, reaching for the same piece of rock.

Oops. I'd been focusing so much on UP, I kind of forgot to notice anything else.

"Move over," Carmen said.

"You move over," I said.

"You're in *my* way," she said.

Our ropes were starting to get tangled up. I could hear someone laughing too. And Fish was still screaming.

"LET'S GO! DON'T FREEZE UP ON ME! KEEP THOSE LINES CLEAN! FOCUS ON THE WALL! SPOT YOUR NEXT HOLD! WHAT ARE YOU DOING, KHATCHADORIAN?"

It was getting harder and harder to focus. In fact, I could barely think at all—and *that's* when I lost track of the whole don't-look-down strategy thing.

One little peek was all it took. As soon as I saw everyone else, way down there on the ground below us, that was it. I went straight to crazy town.

It all happened just like the last time. First everything around me kind of went away.

My head started spinning.

My heart started racing like NASCAR.

My face felt about a million degrees hot.

And I heard that rushing sound in my ears.

"Hey, Rafe?" someone said.

It was Carmen. She was still right there—waiting for me to get out of her way. I'd totally forgotten.

"Huh?" I said.

"You know what my brother does when he wants to get my butt in gear?" she said.

"I...don't...really...feel like...guessing games... right now!" I said.

"That's okay," Carmen said. Then out of nowhere, she reached over and pinched me. Hard. It felt like a pair of pliers in my side.

"OUCH!" I yelled. "What do you think you're—?"

"Move," she said.

"I can't!" I said. I wanted to, but I couldn't. As far as I could tell, I was going to be finishing middle school right there, because I wasn't going anywhere. Maybe ever.

"Don't be a wuss," Carmen said. And then she pinched me again—in the exact same spot, but harder.

"STOP IT!!" I yelled at her.

"Make me," she said. And then she did it again.

This time, that pinch felt more like a piranha taking a bite out of my side.

And it was Ticking. Me. Off!

Which I guess was the whole point. I started climbing just to get away from her. I don't really know how—I just moved. I was climbing again, straight up, and not stopping, and definitely, definitely, NOT looking down this time. I'd learned that lesson, and I didn't think my side could take another pinch.

Carmen was crazy, that's for sure. Carmen was dangerous too. And mean. I'd say that ninety-nine percent of the time, Carmen was just looking out for Carmen.

But guess what else? I think I'd just met the other one percent.

And that part was some kind of crazy-dangerous evil genius.

CHAPTER 42

THANKS, I GUESS?

I'm not going to say I *liked* the rest of that climb, but I reached the top, anyway.

Coming back down was another question. We were supposed to rappel, which looked totally cool when everyone else did it. In my case, it looked more like Sergeant Fish lowering a hundred-pound bag of half-frozen peas to the ground.

D.J. was still laughing when I got down there. Burp and Thea asked me if I was okay, but everyone else just looked like they felt sorry for me, including Pittman. Fish didn't say one word.

Mostly, I just wanted to find a hole, crawl inside, and never come out. But first I went over to talk to Carmen. She was sitting on a log and drinking some water when I caught up to her.

"Hey, Carmen?" I said.

"What?" she said.

"Just, um…thanks," I said. "You saved my butt up there."

"You're welcome," she said. "You can pay me back by packing up my gear."

And here's where it got weird again.

"I don't think so," I told her. "You can pack your own gear this time."

Do you ever say something before you even realize it's about to come out of your mouth? I mean, that happens to me all the time. But this time was different.

Carmen looked as surprised as I was. When she stood up, I got that goose-bumpy feeling again. Not the good kind. More like the brace-for-impact kind.

But even though I'd gotten chewed up and spit out on Devil's Highway, I also felt just a tiny bit like I could do anything after that.

Anything. Including this.

"Didn't you just say I saved your butt up there?" Carmen asked, circling toward me.

"Yeah," I said. "And if it weren't for me, you wouldn't even be here anymore. So I'd say we're even."

I think I heard some fingers curling into a fist. I definitely saw her eyes move. She was checking to see where Pittman and Fish were.

And then she stepped off. She didn't say anything at all. She just walked away and started talking to Veronica instead. Later, when it was time to go, she even packed her own gear.

Did I think that meant this was over? Hardly.

Was I still expecting Carmen to push me down a canyon, or smother me in my sleep? Maybe, a little. I wouldn't put it past her.

But at least I'd lived to see another day. And sometimes out there in the wilderness, that's the most you can hope for.

CHAPTER 43

THE MARATHON

After that horrible, terrible, embarrassing climb on Devil's Highway, the next couple of days went kind of...okay. And fast too.

We were pretty much running that camp by ourselves now—getting up, making the fire, cooking the food, breaking down the shelters, and everything in between. D.J. and I even got an extra tag each for putting up Pittman's and Fish's tents. Everything seemed to be pretty much smooth sailing.

I still felt bad for Arnie, getting kicked out like he did, but you know what? Because of him, I think we all worked even harder. Nobody wanted to get the boot this time.

We also had three more obstacles to go—each one good for another tag.

Day five was all about hiking. Pittman and Fish called it the Marathon, which it basically was.

That started with a big trek *up* one side of a mountain. It took us off trail—way off trail. Pittman said we were above the burn zone, which meant we couldn't have any fires up there.

I think we were also above the every-living-creature zone. There weren't any animals. Or even bugs. Unless you counted us cockroaches. And I think the air was getting thinner, because that pack of mine felt heavier with every step.

On our way back down to earth, though, we started seeing a whole bunch of cool animals. There were mountain goats, and marmots, and deer, and rams. Pittman and Fish knew all about them and pointed out some birds too, like the blue grouse, the American dipper, and (okay, this was pretty cool) a real live American bald eagle.

PLEASE FEED THE ANIMALS

GOT GARBAGE?

But we still weren't done with the Marathon, which, it turned out, was two obstacles in one. Next up, Pittman and Fish started handing out blindfolds for something called a trust hike. The idea was to follow someone else along the trail for a mile, even though you couldn't see.

With Arnie out of the picture, we had to work in groups of two and three. Carmen went right for Burp and Thea. I guess that meant she wasn't going to be talking to me if I wasn't going to be doing her work for her. I got paired with Veronica, which seemed like a good thing—at first.

The next morning, we worked like dogs—again—to clear part of the trail and "leave it better than we found it." (I think that was Captain Crowder's theme song.)

By the time we finished fixing the trail, hiked back to our campsite, and sat down for "lunch" (peanut butter and crackers, plus whatever peanut butter you could lick off your fingers), everyone was worn OUT. I was ready for a vacation—not that I was about to get one.

Five and a half days down. Nineteen tags earned. Eight obstacles completed.

That meant one more obstacle to go before we hit the home stretch.

And this one wasn't going to be like any of the others.

CHAPTER 44

JUST ONE MORE

One more to go, cockroaches. Not too shabby," Fish said, right before they started handing out the paper and pencils again.

"Another quiz?" Carmen said as the other kids started to groan.

"Nope," Pittman said. "These materials are all you'll be taking with you this afternoon on your solos."

"Our what-o's?" Burp said.

"Solos," Pittman said. "As in—on your own. It's a time for you to sit quietly by yourself and reflect on what you want to take away from this experience."

When I got my paper, I saw it was just a blank sheet.

"I don't get it," D.J. said. "What are these for?"

Fish took that one. "Each of you *will* use this time to write yourself a letter. In that letter, you *will* answer one question. And that question is: What do you want your life to look like one year from today? Think hard about it.

"At the end of your solos, when you've shown us that you've written a *real* letter, you will seal it in an envelope, address it to yourself, and hand it back to me. Then, one year from today, you can expect some mail."

"Ooh, super-deep," Carmen said with a snicker.

"Stow it, Carmen," Fish said.

"How long do these solo things last?" Burp asked.

"All afternoon," Fish said.

"And what do you mean, a *real* letter?" Diego said.

"We mean actual sentences. We mean more than one paragraph," Pittman told us. "We do *not* mean writing *I am so bored* over and over on your page."

"Anyone who chooses to not write the letter, or spends his or her solo goofing off, can expect to be packing his or her bags this evening," Fish said. "My suggestion is—take it seriously, cockroaches."

That's when I started to figure out why this all felt kind of familiar. Hours of sitting there, alone, with nothing to do but some kind of homework? Yeah, I'd done this before, all right. In school. And more than once.

Maybe they called it a solo, but I knew was it really was.

This was an in-woods suspension.

CHAPTER 45

SOLO ARTiST

Pittman and Fish walked us way up into the
woods and dropped us off in different spots
where we couldn't see or hear each other. They
said they'd be patrolling the area, so "don't think
about any funny business." At the end of the time,
Pittman was going to blow an air horn, and we
were all supposed to make our way back to camp.

Meanwhile, it was just as bad as I thought.
It was pretty creepily quiet out there. Just me,
the woods, a piece of paper, a pencil, and my own
thoughts.

I stared at that empty page. I tried to think
about what I wanted to put in that letter to myself.
Then I started to write.

Dear Rafe

That's as far as I got. I couldn't think of anything else to say, and even worse, I *really* didn't feel like figuring it out.

So I stared at the sky and the trees for a while.

I watched an ant take forever to carry a piece of leaf about two feet.

After that, I looked at my letter some more. I put a comma after the "Dear Rafe" part.

Then I took another stare-at-the-sky break.

Somewhere in there, I finally figured something else out. I didn't need both sides of that page just for a little letter. And there was no sense letting the other side go to waste.

So I flipped it over, put it down on the flattest rock I could find, and started to draw.

CHAPTER 46

SOLO, SO LOW, WHAT'S THE DIFFERENCE?

I still had a million more minutes to go out there. Or two hours. Or thirty seconds. I had no idea. At least with in-school suspension, you know how long you're going to be there.

Now I didn't even have a clock tick-tocking me toward the finish line. But the funny thing was, after a while, it started to feel like I did. I could have *sworn* I heard it, going by in slow motion. Tick...tock...tick...

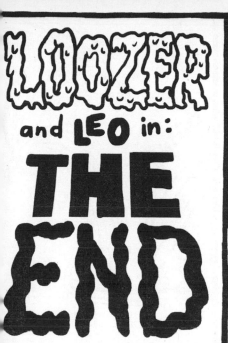

CHAPTER 47

DEAR COCKROACH

When I'd stalled as much as I could, I started to panic. The shadows of the trees were getting longer and longer in the afternoon sun.

What was the question again? Oh yeah— what I want my life to look like a year from now.

Hmm, what I really want is to somehow win ten million bucks, live in a huge mansion far, far away from Hills Village, with a whole wing for my mom and Grandma Dotty. Don't worry, I didn't forget about Georgia. I'd give her a job at one of my many theme parks, scraping bird poop off the benches.

But I have a feeling that's not the kind of letter Sergeant Fish wanted.

So I just started writing. And you know what? Future Rafe wasn't a bad person to write to. I had a feeling he knew exactly what I was trying to say.

Dear Rafe-One-Year-from-Today,

Hi. How are you doing? How's life going in the future? Remember when you were sitting in the woods writing this? That probably seems like a long time ago, doesn't it? Not to me. I'm still stuck here. In fact, I wish I was you.

I mean, I know I _am_ you, but just not yet. (Man, your head could explode thinking about this stuff!)

ANYWAY, I'm supposed to answer this one question: <u>What do I want my life to be like one year from today?</u> I don't know how much longer this <u>solo thing</u> is supposed to last, so I better come up with something quick. Okay, here's what I want:

One year from now, I want to be back in my regular life, but better. I know that means going to Hills Village Middle School, but if it makes Mom happy, then that's a good thing.

I want to be getting all A's and B's in school. Okay, maybe ~~one C~~ three C's, tops. But no D's and definitely no F's.

I want to be making cool art. All the time.

And as long as I'm asking, I want Mom to sell at least ~~one~~ five of her own paintings. Maybe she could also meet some guy who will be nice to her and take her out for dinner sometime. But only if he's _really_ nice.

Grandma Dotty deserves a boyfriend too, I guess, but that's just gross. So maybe she can win a trip to Hawaii or something.

And Georgia's really smart, so she deserves to get a scholarship to any boarding school she wants. In any state she wants. <u>Except</u> for the one I live in.

Last (but this one's important), one year from today, I want to be thinking about how glad I am that I never, ever, EVER have to spend another week in the middle of nowhere with Sergeants Pittman and Fish, especially Fish, ever again.

I guess that's it. See you in a year. Good luck!

Your ~~friend,~~ self

Rafe

CHAPTER 48

A CELEBRATION OF SORTS

I guess everyone else wrote actual letters too, because that night, we had a celebration. *Of sorts.* That's what Fish said, since we weren't done yet. But they brought out the graham crackers, marshmallows, and real live actual Hershey bars from wherever they'd been hiding them. Then we had the best s'mores in the history of the universe of s'mores.

We even had this dinky little ceremony around the fire. Fish and Pittman said we'd all earned the right to run the last day of the course, and handed out our twentieth tags.

Right before they made us give all our tags back.

"You don't need them," Pittman said. "It's the memories you'll keep. Those are more valuable than anything."

I guess that meant Captain Crowder was too cheap to buy new string, washers, and paint every time.

But who cared? Not me. We were *this* close to being done. That meant no more tags to earn. No more shelters to build. No more "Move-move-move-move-MOOOOOOVE!" in the morning. I felt like I was home free.

Even if I wasn't. Not yet.

We kept asking Pittman and Fish what the last day was all about, but they weren't telling.

"I'll say this much," Pittman said. "You all need to be ready for anything."

"It's the *last* day, not a *free* day," Fish said. "Just the opposite, cockroaches." He even smiled when he said it, which sent a chill down my spine.

I don't know why I thought anything was going to get easier around there. Maybe it was those s'mores, making me sugar crazy or something. But I was dead wrong.

If anything, it was going to get s'more worse before it got s'more better.

CHAPTER 49

GONE!

When I woke up the next morning, camp seemed kind of quiet.

And then I realized why. It *was* quiet. That's because Fish wasn't screaming us awake at the crack of dawn.

In fact, dawn had already cracked.

"What's going on?" I said when I came outside.

"Fish and Pittman are *gone*," Thea said. You could see where their tents had been—but no tents now. Just a couple of Sarge-shaped dents in the ground.

"Hey!" Diego said. "What's that?"

When I looked where he was pointing, I saw a note stuck into a big pine tree with a Swiss Army knife.

"*Fish*," I said. It had to be.

D.J. got to it first and ripped it down. The rest of us all huddled around while he read it out loud.

Good Morning!

I will start by telling you a secret: Cockroaches are survivors. There is not much in this world tougher than one of those little guys. They were here long before we were and they will be here long after we're gone.

So never fail to respect the cockroach, cockroaches. And wear the title with pride. You've almost earned the right to keep it for life.

From here, you will travel 3.2 miles northeast along the marked Highline Trail to the next checkpoint. Use your compass, fire starter, and team skills to navigate successfully past the checkpoint and on to base camp.

Further instructions are on the back of this note. DO NOT DIVERGE FROM THE INSTRUCTIONS. If you wish to successfully complete this program, you will work as a team and do everything you're told.

Don't blow it now,
Sgt. F. R. Fish

P.S. Just because you can't see us doesn't mean you're not being watched.

Everyone stopped at the same time and looked around. Did that mean Pittman and Fish were out there somewhere?

Probably. And by *probably*, I mean, of course they were.

Thea took the note out of D.J.'s hand and turned it over. That's where the rest of the instructions were.

"Break down camp per normal," she said. "Pack gear per normal. Follow the markers to the head of the Highline Trail."

"What's 'pernormal'?" Burp said. "Is that like abnormal?"

"*You're* abnormal," D.J. said.

"Shut up, Burp," Burp said. "I mean—shut up, D.J."

"Everyone shut up," Thea said. "It says here—"

"Since when are you in charge?" Carmen asked her.

"Why? You think *you're* in charge?" D.J. asked Carmen.

"Can't we just focus and try to get out of here?!" Thea broke in. "I don't know about you guys, but I want to go home."

There was something about that word—*home*. It seemed like everyone heard it and figured out that Thea was right. The one thing we all wanted was to get out of there. But first we had to escape. The only way to do that was to start moving.

"Okay, let's do this," Burp said.

"We *can* do this," Thea said.

"Do we have any choice?" Carmen said.

And that's when it started to rain.

CHAPTER 50

NO *I* iN TEAM

Watch out!"

"You watch out!"

"I'm trying to let you go first. So GO!"

"Calm down."

"YOU calm down!"

I guess you could say it wasn't going so great. The rain kind of stunk, but then again, so did we. At least we got a shower out of it.

When we finally got to the checkpoint, it was just an old campground. There was a fire circle made out of rocks, and in the middle of that, someone had left three cans of baked beans, which I guess were better than the oatmeal, or at least better than nothing.

There was a note with the cans too. It was all wet and runny, but we could still read it.

When the beans are hot, you may eat them for lunch. Then, and only then, you may retrieve your next instructions. (Look up.)

Over our heads, there was another note, hanging on a string, on a branch, way up high. I guess we had to figure out how to get it down.

"One thing at a time," Thea said. "First we need a fire for those beans."

"Yeah, well, that's not going to happen," D.J. said. "Hello? *IT'S RAINING!!*"

He turned around in a circle and yelled that last part a couple times. To make sure Fish and

Pittman heard him, I guess. It was weird, knowing they were out there somewhere, stalking us. Like wolves. Or zombies. Or wolf-zombies.

"Can we just eat the beans and go?" Burp said.

"Dude, we *have* to make a fire. It says so right here," Diego said. "I'm not blowing this now."

"Me either," Thea said. Veronica was nodding. None of us wanted to ignore *any* of Fish's instructions, just in case.

"There's got to be some wood we can burn around here," Diego said. After the first thunderstorm, Pittman and Fish had shown us how to find dry logs under evergreens and pull dead branches off trees with a rope.

"Yeah, but we still need something for tinder," D.J. said. "Wet birch bark's not going to cut it. Not out here IN THE RAIN!!!"

"Yeah, yeah, they heard you the first ten times," Burp said.

"Shut up, Burp."

"No, YOU shut up."

"BOTH OF YOU SHUT UP!"

It was Fish's voice. It came from somewhere

behind me, but I swear when we turned to look, there wasn't anybody there.

Before anyone could say anything else, Carmen spoke up.

"We can use Rafe's notebook," she said, pointing at me.

"What notebook?" Thea said, whirling around.

"The one he's been writing in all this week."

"Not writing. Drawing," I said as everyone gathered closer.

"Writing, drawing, it all burns the same," Carmen said. She was looking right at me now. It was like her eyes had a message for me, and the message was: *GOTCHA*. She hadn't forgotten what had gone down, and I guess she'd been waiting to make her move.

"No way," I said. "It's *my* notebook."

"Just some blank pages," Diego said. "Not all of it."

"I don't have any blank pages," I said. I was already drawing on the back of everything I had.

But now it wasn't just Carmen looking at me like a creep. Everyone was. They all wanted that notebook now.

And here's the thing. Maybe Carmen was evil, and mean, and crazy, and dangerous. But she was also right. We needed that fire, and I couldn't think of any other way to do it.

I mean, it wasn't like I'd forget those comics. I could always redraw them. But it *was* like Carmen getting in the last word. Or the last punch. Whatever you want to call that, it felt a whole lot like *losing*.

So while everyone looked for dry logs, and started making a little fire shelter, and got out the frying pan and can opener from D.J.'s pack, I started figuring out which Loozer comics had to go.

Once everything was set up, I used the flint and fire starter from D.J.'s pack to get a spark going. It took a while, but then the paper started to burn.

"Yes!" Thea shouted.

Watching that fire was like the definition of mixed feelings for me—like Jeanne Galletta telling me I'm the *second*-coolest guy in school.

"Thanks, Rafe," Burp said.

"Yeah, dude. We totally appreciate it," Diego said as he huddled closer to the flames to warm up. I'd gone from Weak Link to Fire Savior, just like that.

Maybe it didn't feel the way I thought it would, but it did get us one big step closer to home. And for right then, that was all that counted.

CHAPTER 51

FULL CIRCLE

After we cooked and ate those beans, it was time to move on.

"What now?" I said.

"Thea, get on my shoulders," D.J. said. "And Veronica, get on her shoulders." Veronica and Thea were *just* light enough that D.J. could support them.

I didn't think it was going to work, but it did. Pretty soon, Veronica was pulling down that envelope and we were reading the note inside.

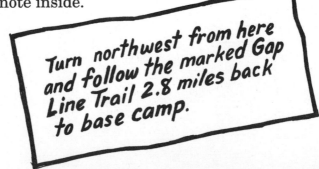

Turn northwest from here and follow the marked Gap Line Trail 2.8 miles back to base camp.

Yes! This was the *real* home stretch—the one I'll bet everyone had been thinking about since we got on that bus a week ago.

Was it really just a week? It felt more like I'd been out there for ten years. And each one of those years was three years long.

Still, we were moving now, and we had a plan. That 2.8 miles went by faster than I thought, and all of a sudden, we were coming out of the woods and into a familiar place.

Straight ahead, I could see that climbing tower from the first day. I didn't even mind the memory of my freak-out, because this time I didn't have to go near it. All I had to do was smile, wave, and keep on moving.

"Hey, look!" Burp said.

A bunch of kids were getting ready to start climbing. When I looked up at the top, I could see that trunk of food waiting for them too. I wondered what was in there, since we never did get to find out.

"Ready?" some other sergeant yelled at them. "Three, two, one—GO!" And those kids started climbing like their lives depended on it. Or at least, their dinner.

"Is that…Arnie?" Thea said.

I looked again, and sure enough, it was him. I guess he got a second chance faster than anyone expected, and he was going for it. He was already yelling at everyone else, telling them how to get to the top.

And I thought, *Good luck, Arnie*. But that was it. None of us stuck around to see how they did. We were on the move too. Running like crazy, straight for base camp and that finish line. We were so close we could smell home.

"Let's go, cockroaches!" Diego yelled, and we all said the next part together, at the same time.

"Move, move, move, move, MOOOOOOVE!"

CHAPTER 52

LATER!

The bus ride from base camp back to civilization was kind of...weird.

I shook hands with Carmen, if you can believe that. I guess I never should have listened to her in the first place. Not that I knew any better. Sure, it seemed like she got in the last word, but at least she hadn't broken my face yet.

Maybe I was learning. Maybe after this, every other girl was going to seem easy to figure out and talk to. Maybe Carmen was as tricky as it got.

"Later, Rafe," she said to me.

"Later," I said back.

"I still think you're kind of cute," she said, which was just about the weirdest part.

And I thought, *Have a nice life, Carmen.* But I

didn't say it out loud. She could still punch me in the throat if she wanted to.

After that, I moved to a different part of the bus.

"What happens to you now?" Burp said. Everyone suddenly wanted to know what everyone else was doing after this.

"Just middle school," I said. "That's it."

It was kind of depressing. A week from that Monday, I was going to be running around HVMS and wishing I was anywhere else. That seemed pretty boring compared to what I'd been doing for the last seven days. I'm not saying I loved every minute of The Program—or *any* minute of it—but you know what else? It was definitely an experience I wouldn't forget.

"What about you?" I asked Burp.

He kind of shrugged. "I've got big plans," he said. "I'm going to be…um…" But then he stopped and thought about it for a second. "Actually, just middle school. Same as you," he said.

"Well, good luck," I said. I meant good luck with his lying problem, but also with the whole middle school thing.

In a way, it felt like we were all going back to

our own war zones. I had Stricker and Stonecase waiting for me, and Miller the Killer, and Jeanne Galletta, and all the other new kids and teachers I didn't even know about yet. Not to mention the math, English, social studies, and science that I *did* know about.

But I also had Mom. And Grandma. And cheeseburgers and apple pie at Swifty's, plus free milk shakes when Swifty made a mistake. And Jeanne Galletta. (She goes on both lists.) And my own bed. And indoor bathrooms. And toilet paper.

And yeah, okay, my sister too. I guess. But only after Mom, Grandma, real food, Jeanne, my bed, bathrooms, and toilet paper.

Because *those* were the things I really missed.

HOME, HOME, HOME, HOME, HOME

You don't need to know about the whole drive home—or about how I kind of, maybe, cried a tiny bit when I hugged Mom hello. But I'm pretty sure she didn't see, and I know Georgia didn't see, or else I'd never hear the end of it.

Hey, what can I say? I love my mom.

And guess what? She's afraid of heights too. I never knew that before, maybe because I never had a reason to ask her. But now that my skydiving, high-rise window washing, and cell phone tower installation careers are on hold, we decided we're going to work on this together. I'm not exactly sure how yet—it's just one more thing I'm going to have to deal with. But I'm glad Mom's on my side.

Meanwhile, I redrew all those comics I'd burned, in the car before we even got back to Hills Village. I wanted to do them while they were still fresh in my memory. In fact, they came out better when I did them a second time. I'll bet Ms. Donatello would like to know that. The last time I was in her class, she was always telling me to redo stuff.

I was even thinking maybe I'd try putting some of those Loozer comics online, just to see what happens. Call me weird if you want, but I felt like I owed Loozer a favor. Poor little dude. He's got enough problems without getting burned and forgotten.

Also meanwhile, it was amazing to get home again. It felt like seeing a whole bunch of old friends for the first time in way, way too long.

265

CHAPTER 54

HELLO, SISTERS

Something else you need to know about—and it's a big one—is that we had our meeting with Mrs. Stricker and Mrs. Stonecase on the Friday before school started.

Mom brought my completion certificate from The Program, so there couldn't be any funny business about *not* letting me back into HVMS.

"I'd like to have this placed in Rafe's file," Mom said. She gave a copy of it to Stricker (no way were we giving up the original), and I was all for that. Because I don't want to get all the way to the end of this book without saying—GUESS WHAT?

Certificate of
COMPLETION
this is to certify that
Rafe Khatchadorian has completed
The Program in a satisfactory
manner.

So at least I was going to be re-enrolled at HVMS. That was good...ish. But we weren't done yet.

"Mrs. Khatchadorian," Stonecase started in. "There is still the matter of Rafe's academic adjustment to discuss before the school year begins."

"Excuse me?" Mom said. "His academic... adjustment?"

I think I felt my eye twitch. Stricker may not have been happy to see me, but there was *something* about this she liked. I could just tell. It was like the old instinct kicking in.

And right now, she was looking at me the way a heavyweight champ looks at a skinny little kid who wandered into the wrong gym.

"Based on Rafe's transcripts before and after he left HVMS," Stricker said, "we'll need to enroll him in some repeat and special classes."

"Repeat?" I said. "Special?"

"We need to be certain he's ready to tackle his grade level before we can actually let him proceed," Stonecase said.

"*Proceed?*" I said. I didn't like the sound of any of those words.

"Believe me, Rafe," Stricker said slowly, "I want you to...*succeed* here just as badly as you want it."

Well, I knew what that meant. She wanted me out of her middle school just as fast as possible. It was the one thing in the universe that Ida P. Stricker and I had in common.

"But," Stricker said, "that may not happen as quickly as we might have liked."

"In other words, Rafe," Stonecase said, "now that

you've made your way back into Hills Village Middle School, there's really no knowing how long it's going to take you to finish. That part will be up to you."

"And…up to me," Stricker said. The way she almost-but-not-quite smiled told me everything. If I was going to make her life miserable, she was going to return the favor—and then some.

I was back, all right.

Way back.

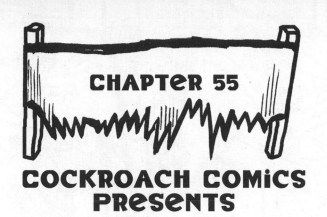

CHAPTER 55

COCKROACH COMICS PRESENTS

So that was my summer. How was yours?

Now that school is starting up again, I've got my hands full, to say the least. But that's another story for another day—and another book. Don't worry, I'm not going anywhere.

Still, one good thing did happen. Or at least, kind of happened. I mean, I'm the only one around here who knows about it, so I'm not sure if that counts. But you can keep a secret, right?

Yeah, that's what I thought.

Later!

HIGH ADVENTURE ON THE HIGH SEAS!

Your sneak peek starts
on the next page!

AVAILABLE NOW

1

Let me tell you about the last time I saw my dad.

We were up on deck, rigging our ship to ride out what looked like a perfect storm.

Well, it was perfect if you were the storm. Not so much if you were the people being tossed around the deck like wet gym socks in a washing machine.

We had just finished taking down and tying off the sails so we could run on bare poles.

"Lash off the wheel!" my dad barked to my big brother, Tailspin Tommy. "Steer her leeward and lock it down!"

"On it!"

Tommy yanked the wheel hard and pointed our bow downwind. He looped a bungee cord through the wheel's wooden spokes to keep us headed in that direction.

"Now get below, boys. Batten down the hatches. Help your sisters man the pumps."

Tommy grabbed hold of whatever he could to steady himself and made his way down into the deckhouse cabin.

Just then, a monster wave lurched over the starboard side of the ship and swept me off my feet. I slid across the slick deck like a hockey puck on ice. I might've gone overboard if my dad hadn't reached down and grabbed me a half second before I became shark bait.

"Time to head downstairs, Bick!" my dad shouted in the raging storm as rain slashed across his face.

"No!" I shouted back. "I want to stay up here and help you."

"You can help me more by staying alive and not

letting *The Lost* go under. Now hurry! Get below."

"B-b-but—"

"Go!"

He gave me a gentle shove to propel me up the tilting deck. When I reached the deckhouse, I grabbed onto a handhold and swung myself around and through the door. Tommy had already headed down to the engine room to help with the bilge pumps.

Suddenly, a giant sledgehammer of salt water slammed into our starboard side and sent the ship tipping wildly to the left. I heard wood creaking. We tilted over so far I fell against the wall while our port side slapped the churning sea.

We were going to capsize. I could tell.

But *The Lost* righted itself instead, the ship tossing and bucking like a very angry beached whale.

I found the floor and shoved the deckhouse hatch shut. I had to press my body up against it. Waves kept pounding against the door. The water definitely wanted me to let it in.

That wasn't going to happen. Not on my watch.

I cranked the door's latch to bolt it tight.

I would, of course, reopen the door the instant my dad finished doing whatever else needed to be done up on deck and made his way aft to the cabin. But, for now, I had to stop *The Lost* from taking on any more water.

If that was even possible.

The sea kept churning. *The Lost* kept lurching. The storm kept sloshing seawater through every crack and crevice it could find.

Me? I started panicking. Because I had a sinking feeling (as in "We're gonna sink!") that this could be the end.

I was about to be drowned at sea.

Is twelve years old too young to die?

Apparently, the Caribbean Sea didn't think so.

READ MORE IN

AVAILABLE NOW

ABOUT THE AUTHOR

JAMES PATTERSON was selected by readers across America as the Children's Choice Book Awards Author of the Year in 2010. He is the internationally bestselling author of the highly praised Middle School books, *Treasure Hunters*, and the I Funny, Confessions, Maximum Ride, Witch & Wizard, Daniel X, and Alex Cross series. His books have sold more than 275 million copies worldwide, making him one of the bestselling authors of all time. He lives in Florida.

CHRIS TEBBETTS has collaborated with James Patterson on three other books in the Middle School series and is also the author of The Viking, a fantasy-adventure series for young readers. He lives in Vermont.

LAURA PARK is a cartoonist and the illustrator of three other books in the Middle School series and the I Funny series. She is the author of the minicomic series *Do Not Disturb My Waking Dream*, and her work has appeared in *The Best American Comics*. She lives in Chicago.